THE
INBETWEEN

KLAUDEN'S RING SAGA

THE
INBETWEEN

AWARD-WINNING AUTHOR
JM PAQUETTE

DEDICATION

For all the in-between places and secret faces that never see print

TABLE OF CONTENTS

I

BLOOD JOURNAL

This story takes place before the events of Klauden's Ring, explaining what happened to make Hannah leave her father's castle in the mountains.

"Why, Klauden, what are you staring at?" Hannah asked, making the question light and flirty, but it fell flat between them, the words too contrived to be truthful. Her intended mate gave her a sardonic look, lust fleeing his face as one ink-stained finger pushed blond hair behind an ear. He sat half-turned in the elegant library chair, one hand perched on the polished wooden arm, the other still resting on the open page of the book he was no longer reading. The magical light from his lamp spilled over the pages and onto the large reading desk, highlighting the angles of his face. The rest of the castle used firelight and torches for illumination, but Klauden was always so careful around the books, only using magical light when he was down in the library.

"I am looking at you, chaivin," the vampire told her, face unreadable again, and her skin prickled at the nickname, the closeness of a childhood spent together echoing in her fingertips. Not for the first time, Hannah wished she had a private name for him, but he was always Klauden van Sherinak, First Son to the Second Family in her father's castle. She couldn't recall when he had started calling her "chaivin," the old word a reference to fire, but she always wondered if it was because of her red hair or what Kelvin Malbrek, their teacher, would call her fiery temperament. Perhaps he had started when she was a baby. Though twenty years separated them, Klauden would have been a child himself then, just learning to read the old tongues. She considered the eighty years of her life spent in this castle, some of it in this very library in the basement watching Klauden and his beloved books, and hoped that the years ahead included more hungry looks from her betrothed. Some old guides did say that the first hundred years was the most exciting century in a marriage.

"Well," she said as the moment stretched out, "at least the servants finally found a dress that you noticed."

Klauden smiled, shaking his head at her. "I always notice," he claimed. "Sometimes I choose not to comment because I know what that would do to your already ridiculous ego."

She glared at him, watching as the sudden heat she had felt in that first look faded, and he was just Klauden again, her friend, her tutor, her confidant, her intended mate. She had known her entire life that she would marry him. Such was her destiny, a decision made by their parents long before she was born. And she had always been glad. Klauden was handsome. He was fun, sometimes, and more importantly, he was here and familiar. She knew that some First Daughters were sent to other castles to marry complete strangers. Hadn't her own mother come from Gerter van Lartner's castle in the east, sent to marry her father, the esteemed Magnus van Kreeosk, when she turned one hundred?

No, her place was here, First Daughter, promised mate to Klauden. Eventually, they would rule the castle as her father did. *Except*, Hannah thought bitterly, *when I take over, I will force Kelvin Malbrek to first lick my fashionable boots before I banish him from this castle entirely*. The magician may be her father's second-in-command, and her own teacher, but he was nothing to her, and she would be glad to see him gone.

Hannah never had been very good at school. Klauden was her savior there, as in other things. He took the time to tutor her, helping her with the magic, explaining so simply the things that Malbrek never seemed to say in a way that made any sense. Klauden always knew just what to say— or when not to say anything at all.

She knew that he was about to dismiss her, turning his attention back to the words he was always reading and dooming her to yet another afternoon doing absolutely nothing, so she moved quickly to stand directly next to the chair he sat in, making sure the dress swished as she did. Klauden paused, his head still elegantly inclined in her direction, but his hands had already resumed their position on the table before him, one hand leaning forward to hold the page open, the other finger poised to trace beneath the line he was reading.

The red satin made a luscious sound as it fell gracefully around her small waist, the waves of fabric highlighting the slight curves Klauden had only recently seemed to notice. The cut of the dress was simple enough, a long skirt topped by a corset that left her shoulders and arms bare. She had watched his reaction to the other women in the castle during the dances, noting how his eyes followed the necklines and bare skin, and while most of her dresses revealed her arms, this was the first time he seemed to notice her skin at all.

But it hadn't been her neckline that he had focused on at all when she walked in the library. It was the sound. She knew that Klauden's hearing was far better than his sight, so she had made a point of slowly walking up behind him when she entered the cavernous room. She had taken careful steps on the carpeted floor, letting the fabric of the dress sway subtly from side to side, her own sensitive ears picking up the sultry sound as she approached. She saw the change in him as he heard her, the slight stiffening of his shoulders, his head cocked ever so slightly to the left, and she knew that if she could see his face, his eyes would be closed as he focused on the sound.

Oh, Klauden, she thought, a wave of appreciation and longing rushing through her, *how well I know you.* And on the heels of that, *I am so very lucky.*

She paused at his side, letting the dress fall into place as she looked down into his face, enjoying the rare advantage of height as his pale blue eyes met hers in a moment of honest intimacy. They had been friends. They had been playmates. But this was something new. Klauden turned his full attention to her, body shifting completely to face her. He had even abandoned his beloved reading, the book discarded on the large reading table without even a paper to mark his place.

Hannah wanted him to keep looking at her like that for the rest of the day. Certainly she was more entertaining than all of those words written by people long dead. Then she remembered his last comment and couldn't stop herself from saying, "I am not vain."

Klauden's gaze traveled down her face to her bare shoulders, her torso encased in the tight satin, and then back up again. "I would never have guessed such a thing, my lady," he said in the perfect tone of the Second Family.

She scoffed, knowing that tone for what it was, complete flattery without honesty, sarcasm disguised as civility. They had long grown out of such niceties when alone, though they often put on a good show around her father and their teacher. Klauden's parents had raised a proper vampire, and he always behaved as such when they were in public. When they were alone, though, as they were more and more often of late, their tone always changed.

"Don't call me that," Hannah snapped, not knowing why the title should bother her at the moment, and she reached out to playfully tap his shoulder.

Klauden stood up, pushing the chair back with a smooth motion, and looked down at her. "As you wish," he said quietly. "But you know that you are lovely," he added. "Come here." His height sometimes surprised her. At barely five feet, Hannah knew everyone was taller than she was, but Klauden didn't tower over her as some of the other men in the castle. He wasn't a small man, but slender built, and his chin rested comfortably on top of her head when he leaned toward her, enfolding her in a deep embrace. His arms were wiry but sure, and Hannah was glad that he wasn't muscle bound like some other men. An image of Vailen van Joosen, First Son of the Third Family, flashed into her mind, his broad chest and thick arms, that wide face starting to sprout a thin ginger fuzz, and she shuddered against Klauden's chest. She was glad that Klauden was to be hers; Vailen would not have been so easy to live with.

She thought of the look on the big boy's face when she had first bested him with her daggers. He would not forget that humiliation, and she had known then that she had not earned only her teacher's approval but also her underling's enmity. She was her father's daughter, after all. Such hatred could be put to use someday. Hannah just hoped she found that purpose before Vailen's slow mind had the time to plot something against her. Such thoughts were common, and she dismissed them, sinking into Klauden's chest.

"Chaivin," he whispered into her hair, pulling her tighter.

Hannah returned the embrace with more enthusiasm than he expected, pressing against him with the full length of her body, and he tried awkwardly to compensate for the movement. He may be First Son, born with a vampire's dexterity, but he was no warrior, and he stumbled, feet tripping over each other as he stepped back into the chair. The ancient wooden seat tipped onto its side under their combined weight, Klauden's arms tangled in Hannah's skirts as he tried to right them both, and they went down in a heap, Hannah's forehead striking Klauden's nose with a crunch that echoed in her skull. The smell of warm blood filled the air, and Hannah struggled against her first impulse to lunge for it, instead focusing on righting her limbs and rearranging her skirts. The scent filled her, the temptation to find the source and satisfy her need strong, and she tried to regain control. Then, Klauden's hand found her bare leg, fingers brushing against the skin of her thigh, and she froze, unable to fight the new desire that ran through her, one closely linked to the rising bloodlust.

Don't be ridiculous! she snapped at her body. *You are no fledgling, subject to spells of uncontrollable bloodfever. You are a pureblood, and you should be able to control yourself by now!*

It had been a long time since she had been at the mercy of her needs, and she closed her eyes, kneeling amid a tumble of skirts, taking a long slow breath to calm her galloping heart. She didn't need to breathe, but the ritual gave her something to focus on. She was aware of a brief chant, and she felt a small surge of power as Klauden used his magic to clean his bloodied nose. There was subtle movement in front of her, and then both of Klauden's hands pressed down hard on her thighs, the firm pressure a comfort against the raging need. There was nothing untoward in his touch. He didn't speak, only held himself there, comforting and soothing as he had always been when she had such episodes in the past. She pictured the ever judgmental eyes of Kelvin Malbrek seeing her now, and the desire flooding through her disappeared in a warm rush of embarrassed heat. Klauden sensed her discomfort and removed his hands, leaning back out of reach, long legs folding beneath him and disappearing under the edge of his red robes.

"Forgive me," he muttered, and Hannah could hear the guilt in his voice.

"It was my fault," she insisted, voice strained as the effects of the blood-fever faded. "I knocked us off balance." Her fangs were huge in her mouth, but she could feel them starting to retract as her pulse slowed, the promise of blood no longer tempting her.

"It is I who have no balance," Klauden countered, and they both laughed, the tense moment broken. Hannah felt empty, the bloodlust having drained her energy.

"True," Hannah chuckled hollowly, finally getting her dress into enough order to stand up. She paused before getting up, giving her head another moment to settle into normalcy, and she snuck a look at his pensive face.

"You have not had an episode like that in quite some time," he said quietly. Hannah looked away, eyes tracing the pattern on the ancient area rug that covered the floor.

"I know," she admitted, feeling the flush as her face reddened. *To lose control like a common fledgling,* she thought miserably, and on the heels of that—*my father would be furious.* "I thought I was done with that."

She recalled a series of such episodes—when Anna had split her forehead against the steps; when Klauden had shattered a glass on his desk with a cascade of books, slicing his arm to the bone—and each time, her betrothed was there, hands pressing into her, calling her back to the moment, calming the fury of her blood. She thought of Anna for a moment, at the curiosity in her stepsister's face, at the questions that her dear friend would never ask, not wanting to upset the delicate balance of their trio, but always seeing everything.

Even though they shared a father, Anna hadn't been subject to such desperate episodes. Neither was Klauden. Hannah was not happy to be reminded of her shortcomings yet again. It was bad enough that she couldn't call her magic without the aid of words; losing control around blood like that was shameful. She had been a child the last time it happened in public, and Hannah knew that if anyone had seen what had just happened, she might have an unfortunate accident sooner rather than later. Magnus van Kreeosk did not have daughters who suffered from bloodfever.

"I just wish I knew why it happened," she said finally, watching the explanations flitter across Klauden's face. In the end, he said nothing, only nodded. She stood up in a rush, skirts swishing, though she barely heard them. She wanted to go back to her rooms, take off this dress, curl up in a corner, and die of embarrassment.

Klauden was still sitting on the rug, one corner of the carpet flipped up, dislodged by their tumble. Hannah was surprised that it was still in one piece. The things in the library were ancient. Sometimes she would touch a book and the corners would crumble. She was careful to never let Klauden see when that happened. He was so particular about the books.

He leaned over to flip the rug back into place, one leg stretched out beneath him, his robe hiked up above his knee to reveal a swath of smooth pale skin, but she stopped him. "Wait, what is that?"

"What is what?" he asked, hand holding the faded red edge.

She pointed at the stone floor beneath the rug, taking a delicate step over his outstretched leg. She lifted the fallen chair and pushed it aside. "That!" she said, kneeling down to trace a faint line in the floor—a line that was way too straight to be the result of the ancient castle settling. Klauden folded his legs under him, adjusted his robes, and peered at it, hands slapping hers away as he traced the air above the crack. At her frown, he said, "There is magic here, chaivin." His brow furrowed with concentration, eyes closed, and then his hand froze, seeming to hit some invisible barrier. "Right... here."

"What is it?" she whispered, not wanting to break his focus but eager for a distraction. Klauden held his hand steady, tensing up a little, and Hannah felt the echo of the magic from where she knelt. Then his hand pressed forward, down to the floor. His fingers traced the line carefully, and he was rewarded with a low snick as something shifted beneath the floor. A small square of stone fell into the new opening, then slid aside, revealing a cubby about four inches deep. There was a book inside.

Hannah scoffed, sitting back. She'd been so excited to find something interesting. She sighed. "Great. Yet another book."

Klauden reached cautiously into the opening, fingers lifting the book gently into the air. Hannah watched with a bored expression. Maybe the book was old enough to disintegrate when the air hit it. That would be somewhat interesting to see. She waited, eyes scanning for the dust trail that would signal the start of the process.

Unfortunately, the book held firm, and Klauden placed it on the rug next to the hole. He peered into the opening again, hands darting inside to pull out a silver necklace, a crude rendering of the moon hung from a thin chain. He held it up, the pendant swinging in the silent library, and held it out to her.

"And a shiny for you, my dear," he offered, and she swatted his hand away.

"I don't want it," she told him, getting to her feet. "It's like a child's trinket."

"People don't take such pains to hide children's toys," he said. "This is old magic."

"Of course it's old magic. Everything down here is ancient. This library is older than my father." She took a few steps away from him, then turned back. He was still looking at the opening, head cocked in that scholar's inquiry that signaled the onset of long hours spent buried in some kind of book. It was a welcome distraction though. She could use some time to herself. She walked over to the table where he had been sitting, pulling his lamp to the edge. She could see in the dark, of course, all purebloods could, but it would require her to call on her nightvision, and with the memory of the bloodlust still tingling in her skin, she didn't think it wise to tempt her senses. The lantern would lend sufficient light to get up the stairs and back to the main level of the castle. From there, she could disappear into her rooms.

She heard the snick as the hidden panel closed and the thump of the carpet as Klauden replaced it. He stood up, taking a few awkward steps toward her, face pressed close to the book already open in his hands. The necklace dangled between his fingers, jangling back and forth as he stepped, bouncing against the red robes he always wore. His eyes were already skimming the words. It always boggled her mind to see how fast he could read.

"Chaivin," he whispered, and though she had expected the distant dismissal of the fascinated scholar, something in his tone made her pause and give him her full attention. "You need to look at this," he added, eyes rising from the page to meet hers.

"Why?" she asked, trying to ignore the frisson of fear that zinged up her spine at that look. "You know I don't enjoy reading."

"You want to read this one, I think."

She sighed, shaking her head and holding out her hand. "Fine," she said, fully expecting him to hand her some tome about the history of tribal mating rituals. "I imagine it will be a scintillating read."

"It might be," Klauden said, holding her gaze as he handed the book over. "It was written by your grandmother."

Hannah sat staring straight ahead, her blurred vision skewing the light from the oil lamp on the low table next to her. It didn't matter if she kept her eyes open or closed anymore, the words had burned themselves across her vision, her grandmother's loopy scrawl pressed hard against the pages of the journal as if forced down by the weight of her secrets.

She had been sitting in the plush chair in the corner of her front room for the better part of two days now. The first day had been spent plowing through the handwritten diary, hands gripping the book with ever increasing fury as she continued to read.

> *I do not care anymore. I know what they would say if they knew, and I know what I would say if it was someone else, but none of that matters. I care no more for the court of public opinion now than I did then, though I realize such cares would probably keep me alive longer. It's only a matter of time, now.*

Hannah shook her head. *Who would think such things?* Hannah scoffed, the sound somewhere between a cough and a sob. *And what moronic imbecile would commit such thoughts to paper?* Hannah was suddenly very glad for her father's good sense—he would never have been so foolish. As for her mother, well, the journal spoke to that very issue.

> *He is so much more than I ever thought possible. I have been so wrong for hundreds of years. And if I have already*

been living my life so poorly, then perhaps what comes next is not such a crime after all. The time has come to put my desires first for once. I will not be sorry for it.

Hannah snorted. As if her grandmother ever wanted for anything. As if the Lady of the First Family of Lartner castle could ever suffer as these words seemed to suggest. The woman should quit her pathetic whining and get on with the business of bringing pride to the family name. Hannah paused at the thought, hearing echoes of her father in it, wondering if she would suddenly understand him so well if she hadn't just learned a mind-blowing secret.

Her mother, the late esteemed Lady Alin van Kreeosk, nee Lady Alin van Lartner, was not actually a van Lartner. Worse than that, she was actually a half-breed; apparently her father, Hannah's grandfather, was a mere human, some wandering rogue with whom Isla had rutted during one of her brief trips beyond the castle proper. Hannah shuddered anew at the thought, wincing as she looked down at her hands, an echo of her mother's small hands, fighting the revulsion at the knowledge that human blood tainted her history.

Hannah had never met her grandparents. Her father was older; his father had been dead for centuries when Hannah was born. There were some whispers that perhaps Magnus had hurried Baron von Kreeosk on to that end, but such talk was common in the castle. Everyone was always speculating. But she still heard the occasional word about her maternal grandparents. According to the gossip, Isla van Lartner was the perfect mate to her husband Gerter; they ruled as First Family in their castle as Hannah's father did here. Hannah was certain that if anyone had even suspected that Alin was not Gerter's child, Isla would be long dead, either publicly executed or privately dealt with. She wasn't certain about the way Gerter van Lartner ran his castle, but she doubted that such a secret would have survived long among her people. Most of the purebloods could read surface thoughts, some gifted enough to see into the depths with some prying. Hannah had spent a good part of her life learning to put walls up in her mind, never thinking anything unless she was alone in her rooms, and even then, sometimes curbing her true feelings. With

Klauden, recently she could be more free—but there was nothing that she could hide from him anyway.

The thought made her stomach lurch anew. What would he think, once he found out? Hannah could not keep the secret, certainly not from him. Hell, she would be lucky to keep it from the others in the castle. She enjoyed certain privileges as First Daughter, special treatment that she had always enjoyed until now, but she was also under constant scrutiny from the others—and not just the other ruling Families. Livenna, her father's other daughter, watched her constantly, and rumor had it that the girl's abilities to see hidden desires would only continue to grow. While Hannah was privileged as the First Daughter to Magnus van Kreeosk, Livenna hovered among the Kargin, the second born sons and daughters who made up the bulk of the people in the castle, second class citizens who could only hope to curry favor with the First Born of the three Families in the castle. It was only a matter of time until Livenna learned the truth. Hannah wanted to have faith in her own cleverness, but she was enough of a pragmatist to know her own limits. She could run circles around Livenna with her daggers, or even with her own version of magic, but Livenna could see into people, and Hannah knew it was just too risky.

What would happen to her then? She didn't think they would execute her, sacrificed to Cairn; it had been her grandmother's folly—not hers. But they would certainly take her position and title. Hannah wondered why that seemed worse, somehow. She assumed that word would travel either way to Gerter van Lartner, and Isla would face her own fate. She couldn't bring herself to care. The woman had brought shame to her entire family—a degradation that now shadowed Hannah as well.

Oh, Klauden, she thought miserably. She felt a sudden stab of hatred for her betrothed, unexpected and shocking—this was all his fault. If he could only learn to leave books alone. Some things were not meant to be read. Or written down at all.

Hannah glared at the book on her lap, hatred finding a new target. How had the book even come to be there? She knew, of course. Alin must have brought it with her when she came to this castle, keeping her mother's secret safe. How had Alin managed to hide among them for so long? Hannah wondered how a half-blood could have survived. She thought of the look on her mother's face when Malbrek led her into her room those final days, haggard with sickness, and a memory that had always been poignantly sad was suddenly laced with rage. Her mother had known, had known what she was, and had said nothing. Granted, Hannah had been a child when her mother died, but surely forty years was enough time to share the secret with her only child, to warn her somehow.

She threw the book across the room, pages fluttering as it thumped to the ground. She knew that she wasn't making any sense. How could she fault her mother for not telling her and hate her grandmother for writing it down? It was too much.

She needed to talk to Klauden. He would know what to do.

But she couldn't bring herself to get up, to leave this chair, never mind this room. She contemplated a move into her bedroom where she could curl up on the bed, but she didn't want to lie down. It would be too easy to curl up into a ball and never move again.

It wasn't uncommon for her to spend days in her rooms, and no one would comment on it, but she had been careful to hide the book under her skirts whenever a servant or slave came in. She had skipped a meal the day before, not interested in the thin man who stood before her, eyes downcast and skin pale. She had always enjoyed taking the blood, but not now. She didn't know if she could control herself in this emotional state. It was one thing to kill the slave—she wasn't in the habit of biting slaves and allowing them to turn—but she thought she might make a mess of things, and that would certainly get around, the news that the normally meticulous Lady van Kreeosk had made sport of her meal. Then people would start paying attention, wondering what had made her shift her habits.

For all that being First Daughter had its privileges, there were moments when she wished she could be invisible.

She wasn't sure how much time had passed when she heard the snick of the secret door open in her bedroom. It was Klauden, of course. They had been using the hidden passages to get to one another's rooms since they were children. She heard the panel slip back into place, and then the slow footsteps of her betrothed as he walked around her bed. The door into his suite of rooms opened into the front room, which he used as a study, and so they spent most of their time in his rooms sitting on the couch and chairs there—well, he behind his desk and she lounging on every piece of furniture until she managed to coax him outside or downstairs or anywhere that didn't involve a book. Though the door was in her bedroom, Klauden was always careful to walk swiftly past her bed, never looking at the canopy-draped place where she slept, not glancing to the side into the small alcove that held her wardrobe, only staring straight ahead at the door as his feet carried him into the front room. She had a few chairs and a couch as well, but her furniture was more luxurious than his. Klauden primarily used the desk and chair in his room; Hannah didn't even have a desk. She preferred softer places to lounge, and her front room displayed her taste, subtle reds and blacks in silks and satins covering the walls.

He pushed aside the curtain that hung between her bedroom and the front room and stepped inside. Hannah wondered if he already knew. How long would it take him to pluck the information from her mind? It wouldn't be hard. She wasn't trying to shield from him; in fact, she wondered if she could hide anything from him even if she tried.

She watched his face, waiting for the telltale sign of revulsion that showed he knew everything. She knew what her father would say when he found out—the disgust that would curl his lip. She waited to see that expression now on Klauden's face. It would be new. Sometimes she had done things that annoyed him or disappointed him—like when she had taken to putting live critters amid the stacks of books on his desk and shrieking with delight when he finally disturbed the creature and it took off, sending piles of books and papers scattering to the floor. She had never seen disgust though. She wondered what it would feel like.

Instead, he merely walked across the room, knelt before where she curled on the chair, and took her hands. She could feel the fine tremble running through him. But underneath that, she sensed something else—a small sense of satisfaction, as if a long standing mystery had suddenly been solved, the final puzzle piece slipped into place. She could almost hear him filing the name away for future research—the rogue named Kerrin who was her maternal grandfather.

"It does not matter," he said finally.

She sighed, a sad smile curving her lips as she squeezed his hands. "You know better than that, Klauden."

He nodded. He seemed to consider for a moment, thoughts racing through his mind. Hannah couldn't get a sense of their nature, but she could sense the tension in him, the carefully controlled way he was considering and discarding solutions to this new situation.

"No one else needs to know," he suggested.

She gave him a pointed look. "You may be able to keep this a secret," she told him, "but not me." She sighed. "I never was very good at building walls." She could see the objection starting to form—he could help her, he could teach her—and she interrupted him. "And if I started building them now, it would only rouse suspicion."

He nodded again. There was another moment, and instead of rushing thoughts, she sensed hesitation instead, as if he was debating whether to share this new theory. Finally, he spoke very carefully. "I could make it so no one would be able to see it in your mind."

She tilted her head. That was something she had not considered. "What do you mean?"

Klauden looked away for a second, then met her gaze full on, his hands perfectly still as he held hers. "I can take control of your mind, just enough to make sure this information stays hidden. No one would ever know."

Hannah jerked her hands out of his. "Klauden!" she accused, horrified. "You can do such things?"

He nodded, a hint of shame quickly eclipsed by pride, then both emotions quickly hidden. "It would not affect anything else, chaivin. I promise. I can be..." he paused, as if searching for the right word, "selective."

She gave him a scathing look. "You will not mess around inside my head, Klauden," she blurted. Something in his face fell then, and Hannah wanted to reassure him. "It's not that I don't trust you," she said quickly. "I do trust you. I know you would do a good job." She paused, trying to explain the outraged horror she felt at the idea of someone else controlling her thoughts, the most secret part of herself. "I just don't want anyone inside my head. I can't."

He sighed, eyes almost pleading with her. "It's the only way to stay," he told her.

She nodded, knowing what her refusal meant. "I can't do it, Klauden, not even if it means I have to leave this place." *And you*, she added silently. *I cannot do this thing even for you.* Shame flooded her then, the awful sense of guilt at failing this critical test of her loyalty. But it wasn't about

Klauden at all or even her life here at the castle. It was about her mind, her very self, and she could not, would not submit that to the control of anyone else, even her beloved confidant.

"Then you should go," he said quietly, standing up.

Hannah reached for his hands, tugging him back down. "I don't want to go," she insisted, "but I have to..." Now it was her turn to struggle for the right words. "I have to remain myself." She peered at him, willing him to understand. "Do you know what I mean?"

Klauden nodded, his face sad, his eyes resigned. "I do." He looked at her for a long moment, face close to hers, and she thought that he might kiss her, but instead, he stood up abruptly, hands slipping from her grasp.

"If you are leaving, then we have some planning to do."

They met in the tunnels deep beneath the castle, ancient passages worn by water and time as much as the passage of people. Hannah knelt on the stone floor, a small brazier placed carefully on the ground before her knees. She placed her grandmother's journal inside the metal container, then leaned back. Klauden sat forward, hands moving above the book, and Hannah felt the small surge of power as he used his magic to light the book on fire. She could see the tension in him, and she knew that part of it was from this last task.

Klauden loved books. Burning the journal made his skin crawl. Even though he had read every word and committed most of it to memory, it still pained him to lose such knowledge, to know that he was now the only one who contained the words, and when he was gone, the information contained in those pages would go with him. Of course, he knew that such was the way of secrets, but it still hurt him to burn a book, regardless of the sound logic behind the action.

Hannah watched the journal burn with far more satisfaction. Words were dangerous, and now even the knowledge of those words was dangerous, and she wished she had never found the damn thing. The thought was fleeting though. Hannah's pragmatism would not allow her to dwell too long on the possibilities of what could have been. This was how things were, and she could not undo the damage.

They sat in silence until the book was ashes, and then Hannah moved her fingers above the remains, the cinders swirling until the brazier held nothing that even resembled a book. Klauden reached into the brazier then, the red glow draining away as he waved his hand, and soon nothing remained but grey soot. Klauden had always been good with fire.

"You are sure about this?" he asked.

She shrugged, adjusting her shoulders in the newly acquired clothing she wore. It had been Klauden's idea to dress as a servant as she left the castle. No one would notice her at all. *How often do you actually look at any of the slaves or servants here?* he had asked her, and she had nodded. *But they all look at you,* he had noted. *They all know your face, and we don't want your father chasing after you before you even make it off the grounds.*

Will he chase me? The question echoed again in her mind, and she didn't know which answer she preferred. It had seemed like the right choice—leaving. She could get away before everyone found out, before everyone knew about her tainted blood, before everyone looked at her the way she knew they would—some gloating, some pitying. She would not endure that. No, it was better to leave now before anyone knew that anything was amiss. Klauden would know, but he was strong-minded. No one would ever get any secrets from him.

She would never get any more secrets from him, Hannah realized, and the thought made her heart sink even further in her chest. It wasn't really a choice, though. Once they knew about her bloodline, Hannah would not be permitted to mate with Klauden. Hannah wondered what would happen to him, if someone from another House would be sent for him. She had a brief flash of Livenna, the tall dark-haired beauty standing tall at Klauden's side, and she clenched her fists.

No, she assured herself. *My father would never allow such things. Just as I would not be allowed to be with him, neither would she.* Livenna might someday mate with a lower ranking family in another House, but Klauden was still First Son of the Second Family; he would require a far superior bloodline. *We are both tainted.* It was profoundly disturbing to suddenly have something in common with her father's other daughter.

"I am sure," she said finally, her voice more certain than she felt. "I have to go," she added firmly, hands tugging the simple brown sweater tighter across her chest. The layers of skirt and shirt were familiar, but the materials were not—the cloth rough against her skin as she moved. The outfit was loose and nondescript, and she was nearly embarrassed to be seen so in front of the man who would have been her mate. He must think her so plain.

Klauden nodded, seeming not to notice her clothes at all as he reached into a pocket of his red robes to withdraw a small pouch. He reached for the now cool brazier and carefully poured the ashes inside the leather bag. He called on his power again as he held the pouch and tied it shut, and then he handed it to Hannah carefully.

"If you ever need me," he said seriously, "use this." At Hannah's raised eyebrow, he continued. "Take it out, pour the ashes, and call for me. I will hear you, and I will come."

"Klauden," she admonished, taking the pouch reluctantly, "I am going south of the mountains. I will be too far away."

He smirked then, and the look transformed into a genuine smile, the first one she had seen since this whole debacle began. "You will never be too far away from me, chaivin."

She returned the smile, and the moment was bittersweet. She would miss him. Yes, she would miss this feeling, but then again, she could not deny the small flame inside her at the thought of leaving everything behind, exploring new places without any rules or expectations. She would not have chosen to leave, but given the circumstances, she was adaptable enough to be excited about the possibilities. Her future was no longer written; she could do anything she wanted.

The only price was leaving Klauden behind.

"Come with me," she said suddenly, the words out before she could stop herself.

She saw the eagerness in him, the desire to throw everything away and join her in exile, but then his face fell as he remembered his responsibilities at the castle. She knew he could not leave his family; it was unfair to ask.

"Never mind," she said quickly. "I know you cannot." The look of gratefulness drowned out everything else on his face, and she felt the sharp pull of regret, of knowing how very well she understood this man, and knowing that in order for him stay himself, he could not leave the castle. Klauden was a good son; he could not abandon his parents, not even for Hannah.

Hannah had a moment of jealousy. Of all the things she would miss about the castle, her father had not even crossed her mind. She was relieved to be free of him. But Klauden was close to his parents. She had seen him bent over a book with his father, the similarity between Jorus van Sherinak and his son striking. Though Klauden had the look of his father, he had his mother's eyes, the warm blue of Keller van Sherinak sharpened in the keen political savvy that had only been polished in her son. Keller was a smart woman, careful in a way that kept her family safe, instilling solid morals in her only son, even doting on her daughter Morenna, though Klauden's younger sister was a member of the Kargin. The van Sherinaks were a good family, and Klauden was a good vampire—he was kind to the slaves, pragmatic about his meals, and politic in his behavior. Hannah could not see him living anywhere but this castle.

They sat in silence for a long time. When Hannah finally looked up again, she met Klauden's eyes. It was near evens; he would be missed if they waited much longer. Hannah rarely attended the public dinner, preferring the privacy of her rooms to the blood-filled glasses of the high table. Evens always seemed like hypocrisy to Hannah, to drink blood from wine glasses as if they had some secret vineyards beyond the castle that grew only grapes instead of humans. She had no qualms about what she was—she drank blood in order to survive, sometimes poured from cuts into a glass, sometimes directly from the skin, but she never let any of the latter live. Making fledglings was not something she wanted any part of. The ceremony of evens always seemed to ignore the reality of their lives. But Hannah knew how very much her father enjoyed evens. It would take some time for her absence to be noted.

Klauden, though, often attended evens with his parents, the time spent reminiscing over the day. It would be suspicious if he was absent on the day that she went missing. It was important that no one suspect he knew about her flight. He had assured her that he could keep such secrets, and now knowing the extent of his mental abilities, she believed him.

"It's time," he said.

"I know," she replied. But she still didn't move.

"Come, chaivin," he encouraged and stood up. He held a hand to her, lifting her to her feet. He reached behind her to grab the backpack resting on the floor and spent a moment helping her into it. The bag was awkward against her shoulders. She wasn't accustomed to such weight, but it was a minor inconvenience. The bag held her belongings, everything that she now owned—of course she would get used to the weight. Perhaps it would be a comfort as she set out into the unknown beyond the mountains. She had a vague sense of geography and history, things that Kelvin Malbrek had drilled into them in Essentials, and she knew enough about the humans to fit in among them, but she knew she would learn much more as she went. She could adapt. She was her father's daughter, after all.

"So, this is it," she said, standing before Klauden in the stone hallway.

"Almost," he said, reaching into a pocket. He held out his hand, a small silver object resting on his palm.

"A ring?" she asked, unwilling to take the small object yet, taking in the arcane markings that scrolled around the outside.

Klauden nodded. "It was made for you. You should have it." He took it in his other hand, and slid the ring onto the third finger of her right hand. "I want you to have it." A wedding ring would have gone on her left hand.

"Klauden," she whispered, not knowing what else to say. "I..."

"Don't," he whispered, one hand caressing her face, tracing the line of her jaw. "Just take it."

She nodded, wanting to remember the feel of his fingers on her skin forever. The weight of the ring on her right hand was new, a reminder of his hold on her that she would bring with her into another life.

He pulled her close then, enfolding her in a tight embrace, the line of his body hard against her, and she rested there as long as she thought possible, and then for another moment more.

"I will miss you," she said when they separated.

"And I you," he replied.

"I just wish..."

"I know."

Hannah took a deep breath then, knowing that her body didn't need the air, but enjoying the comfort of the motion anyway. "Okay," she said firmly. "Let's do this."

Klauden walked with her to the small wooden door that led to the labyrinth of canyons below the castle, the small paths that wound out of the mountains into the foothills. He opened the door for her, and when she stepped through, he did not follow.

She turned around to face him, his tall frame silhouetted in the doorframe. "Goodbye Klauden."

"Fare thee well, Hannah," Klauden said, the formal blessing for a journey.

Hannah nodded, glad that he had used her name, something reserved for the most sober occasions. Then she turned around and began walking away from the castle.

When she reached the first turn in the stone canyon, she looked back. The small wooden door into the castle was closed.

II

The Warrior

This story takes place during Klauden's Ring, chronicling what happens when Rory returns to Firene after thinking Hannah is dead in Kalford. The first part of these events is included in Klauden's Ring, but this is the entire story.

Rory Tallerin had been riding for three days, trading out his exhausted horse at a farm up the river from Warin, a stop along the Marin River for those who kept the trade routes from Upsen to the northern lands. He was heading back toward Firene and knew he would have to veer to the east soon, or risk capture, and then probably death. He considered for a time if his death would be such a great loss—to Firene, to the royal family there, to his few remaining friends, or to himself.

He had been dreaming, of course. Even while riding, his body knew what to do, his unconscious mind taking over what had to be done to keep the horse pointed north and keep his body on the beast's back. His conscious mind had been elsewhere, searching, scanning, looking ... and finding nothing.

Maybe it wasn't so odd, he considered, since Hannah was a born vampire. It had always been his knack to find people in dreams, to focus on a person and draw his mind close to that soul, wherever it lingered, but Hannah wasn't an ordinary person.

He had spoken to Galina, his wife, just the once, days before she had finally given in to her despair. That had been a conversation worthy of memory, but Rory still wished he could forget. Even after all these years, he was still angry with her. Though for all the grief she had caused him, and he her, he reflected sourly, Galina had been easy to find.

Hannah was proving to be much more difficult. He had been reaching for her, calling to her, wishing he could find her by recalling her face, her eyes, the scent of her skin, the way she always grinned in the midst of battle, a certain familiar bloodlust lurking behind her gaze. Sometimes the pictures helped him to focus; sometimes they shattered his concentration. It was useless. He would never find her. He would never get to say goodbye the right way.

The new horse jumped a fallen trunk across the path along the river, jarring him back to reality. There had been a bad storm up here, perhaps a month ago judging by the overgrown look of most of the fallen trunks.

Rory wondered if it was the same storm they had weathered that night in the cave, the night he had comforted Hannah in her nightmare, the night he had first considered her as anything except another traveling companion in a long line of companions over the years. The horse landed smoothly, but the move made his vest bump against his chest, the soft thump of the folded paper in the vest's inner pocket a reminder that he hadn't needed.

He still didn't know what to make of the map. Obviously, Hannah had left it for him, a clue of some sort to her whereabouts. It had been resting carefully on top of his bag when he woke alone in the room.

His head had been fuzzy, his mind coated in a strange haze that left a bad taste in his mouth; he wasn't positive, but he thought something magical had happened to him. It had to be some sort of spell, a sleep or a charm, that had kept him from noticing Hannah's departure. What worried him was who had cast it. Maybe Hannah had spelled him and left, but then why leave the map?

He slowed the horse to a trot, pulling the worn page from his pocket and unfolding it. He knew where it led. Anyone could decipher the little crosshatches that resembled mountains, the swirls of treetops that represented the endless forest, the wavy lines of the Marin River and several tributaries.

What the average person would not recognize, however, was the small square near the top of the page, the black mark labeled Kreeosk. His eyes traced the page, the clearly delineated line running from Kalford, a city never visible on any map Rory had ever seen, up along the riverside and across the foothills, through the Vanya Mountains, around several clearly posted "routes to avoid" and "potential hazards" to a castle that could only belong to Hannah's father.

He thought he recognized the spiky handwriting, but couldn't recall if it belonged to Hannah or not. He thought he had seen it in her spellbook. He folded the map again, the thought that had plagued him resurfacing.

If Hannah is dead, why would she leave me a map to her father's castle?

It made sense to think that the reason was because she wasn't dead but had been captured instead and was even now being dragged back to her homeland. The possibility was compounded by the fact that he couldn't find her soul, not anywhere in any of the realms beyond that he searched in his mind.

Still, dreamwalking was only Rory's knack; he hadn't any true skill in the area. He clung to the knowledge that before, whenever he had looked for someone, he had found the soul quite easily. And, he thought, he and Hannah had a tie, more of a bond than any he had shared with Galina, so she should be even easier to find.

And yet three days of nothing.

He was fairly certain, despite the ring he now wore on a chain around his neck, that Hannah was not dead at all. Even if they had killed her body, there were other ways of living, other planes of existence, and if Hannah was in one of those places, he would find her. He had to.

It had been a long time since he had felt such a drive to do anything. These past few decades of aimless drifting had passed in a blur; the only thing that had caused him to notice the world at all had been Hannah's cautious smiles, her blunt questions, her quirks and curiosity.

So, is that it then? Am I risking life and limb heading back to Firene because I am that desperate for a purpose again?

He wasn't sure, not yet. All that he was sure of was that Hannah might still be out there, and he had to find her. He had to know what had happened, at least. And if he couldn't find her, then he knew who could.

Caganasti was an old friend, a recluse who lived in Firene, running an odd shop of magical items, spells, artifacts, weapons, and anything else he could find or trade for. The elf had been roosting in his store for at least two hundred years, his clientele the eager young elves seeking adventure and wishing to arm themselves as best they could. Caganasti was the one to see for any and all magical questions, not to mention his reasonable rates for identifying any found items.

The elf was also a renowned dreamwalker.

If anyone could find Hannah, it was his old friend. Rory just hoped it was worth the price. It wasn't that Caganasti would charge him a lot, though he might relieve Rory of a few gold coins. The money wasn't an issue; it never was. Rory had left Firene well taken care of. The trouble was getting to Caganasti without getting caught. Even if they didn't keep their promise and kill him for returning, they would certainly hold him for some time, and that was a delay he couldn't afford, not if Hannah was on her way even now to the mountains.

If Caganasti could find her, which he would, Rory assured himself, he would, then Rory would follow the map to the northwest. Something in him wanted to follow it anyway, skipping the stop in Firene and charging headlong into battle. Of course, it wouldn't help Hannah, if she could still be helped, for him to get himself killed before he even got there. Caganasti knew other things as well, and one of those areas of knowledge was life beyond the Vanya, west of the dwarven mines and in the unknown territories. Such knowledge might make the difference between salvation and disaster.

Okay then, he decided. *It's time to go home.*

Spurring the horse faster, Rory made it to the outskirts of Firene in ten days and four more horses. He paused on the hill just out of sight of Valerius' Temple. As he stood overlooking the white city far below, a strange urgent homesickness filled him, and he shoved it back down. Now was not the time for such reminiscing. There was work to be done.

He withdrew the cloak from his bag, tugging the hood over his head, and prepared to lead the newest horse past the temple and down the hill into the city. Caganasti's shop was on the eastern edge near the walls, situated perfectly between the lower ward and the city proper, but Rory would still have to pass through the guards at the gate without comment.

It had been a long time, he thought; maybe they had forgotten what he looked like. He knew it was a foolish wish, as he started down the path. He had trained most of the guards personally, and the likelihood of a new soldier being assigned guard duty at one of the main gates was unlikely. No, he would know the guards, and they might know him. He had to disguise himself.

Disguise... he thought, then recalled a night long ago, playing an endless game of dice with Kal Langford, and the man explaining how, on one of his many misadventures, he had snuck into a house by pretending to be a servant—a one-eyed servant. This hadn't worked out so well for Kal, seeing as the lady of the house had been quite a lonely one, this tale had gone on to proclaim, and Rory remembered the eye patch Kal had shown him, the black scrap Kal had lost on the next roll of dice. A little piece of sewn cloth laced with a minor charm to make the wearer very unappealing. Kal had suggested that this hadn't worked so well on his new lady friend, but Rory thought it would probably work among his own people.

All he had to do was pretend to be scarred, which he was, and maimed, which the eye patch would suggest. Firenians prided themselves on physical beauty; the wounded and less than beautiful were not looked well upon in society. In fact, Rory recalled, those who were really unappealing were generally not seen at all. With such long lives, there was a lot of time for elves to be scarred, their strong life forces allowing them to survive wounds that would kill most humans. The hypocrisy of ostracizing those who had survived was just one of hundreds of his people's customs that he had never been quite comfortable with. It was terribly convenient now, though. If Rory pretended to be such an unfortunate victim, it was highly unlikely that anyone would notice him.

He tugged the eye patch from the bottom of the bag, thankful once more for the magical spell that allowed the small knapsack to contain much more than the naked eye would assume. Such extraplanar holding spaces were convenient for a traveler like him, and Lira had known that when she gave him the bag when they first met in Galan. *Now there is a good woman,* he thought, securing the strap around his head and tugging up his hood again. Lira was a rare gem among Elven women who normally squeaked at every little inconvenience and complained at every single hardship. *Well, maybe not all Elven women are like that,* he conceded, *but*

Galina was certainly a handful. Not for the first time, he wondered if he would have found the road away from her even if everything hadn't happened like it did.

He made his way down to the eastern gate, falling in line with the few carts and horse-drawn wagons that also sought entrance to the city. For all the destruction that had ravaged the eastern forest and villages like Galan and Talperin, Rory noted, Firene was utterly untouched. He wondered if the goblin hordes hadn't made it this far quite yet, or if they had thought better of facing the Elven army and turned south instead. Whatever the reason, Rory was grateful; it made traveling this way much faster. If Hannah was also heading north, he hoped she had taken the long way around.

Rory stepped up behind a drover with a cart full of hay. He observed the two guards on duty, men he had known well once upon a time, careful to see their faces in brief snatches that would not detract from his appearance as bedraggled Elven traveler.

"State your business," said Byrum in a bored voice. His face was older now, Rory saw, creased with sun and wind, but the daredevil boy was still hiding in there somewhere, beyond the monotonous duty of guarding the gates from threats that never materialized.

"Just a traveler seeking rest, my lord," Rory said in a low voice, head down and shoulders slumped.

Byrum gave him a cursory examination, eyes skidding away from what must be a frightening face to take in his weathered bag and exhausted horse. His partner on duty, a rather scruffy looking elf named Kienar, was studying his fingernails with great interest. Rory remembered reprimanding the man on more than one occasion for his laziness.

"A traveler from where?" Byrum asked, something about his tone forcing Rory to tense ever so slightly.

"Upsen," Rory answered without thinking, still avoiding the guard's face.

"Been a long time since I was in Upsen," Byrum commented. "Is Gregor still the mayor then?"

Rory squeezed his remaining eye shut. Of course, they would ask something like that. It was what he had trained them to do. Where was his mind today? Rory hadn't been to Upsen in many years and had no idea who was mayor now. Byrum had always been a bright student. Rory was trying to calculate the odds of slipping past them into the city without killing them, when Kienar spoke sharply. "Honestly, Byrum, you'd think you were the one up for some leave time. You haven't been anywhere but this city in a hundred years, and you're never going to." He turned bored eyes to Rory, who stood waiting for judgment. "Go on then, sir. Enjoy your stay in our fine city."

Rory took a step away, listening to Kienar shout at someone behind him, "Hey, you can't bring those goats in here!" He wondered if it could really be this easy. He had taken half a dozen steps when someone tapped his shoulder. Rory paused, turning to face the guard he had trained too well. Byrum peered at him intently, his head slowly nodding.

"I knew it was you," the guard said. "I knew you would come back some day."

Rory contemplated feigning confusion but knew it was hopeless. "I'm not here for that," he settled for saying, willing Byrum to believe him.

"You are forbidden to enter the city," Byrum said, his face unflinching.

"Byrum, listen to me. I'm not here to cause trouble. I just need to see an old friend."

Byrum snorted, glancing back at Kienar, then to his former teacher. He shook his head. "You should have written a letter, Tallerin." He looked back toward the guard post, ready to raise the alarm.

Rory tried to think of what might sway the elf, realized that anything he might say would fall against the teachings he had so carefully laid down. He was a victim of his own thoroughness. Still, he had to try. Byrum had always had a soft spot for the innocent, hadn't he? "If you hold me here, an innocent person will suffer."

Byrum paused, mouth open. "What innocent person?"

"It doesn't matter."

His face closed. "Then it doesn't matter to me." He opened his mouth again.

Fine, Rory thought. *If sympathy won't work, perhaps honesty will.* "If you hold me here, I will kill you." At the look on Byrum's still young face, Rory added, "I just need a little time inside the walls. Two hours at the most. Then you'll never see me again. I swear it."

He could see Byrum struggling between his duty and his loyalty to an old comrade. Finally, the elf closed his eyes, gesturing into the streets. "You have thirty seconds," he allowed, then added, "Sir."

Rory nodded his thanks, then took off down the street at a run. He was turning his third corner when he heard Byrum begin shouting for the rest of the guards. He tugged up his hood after discarding the eyepatch—it wouldn't do him any more good now that they were looking for him—determined to make it to Caganasti's before they caught up to him.

The city hadn't changed much, he noted as he ducked behind a wagon filled with bales of hay and watched a small contingent of guards head towards the gate. It was still the same sprawl of white buildings, some a bit gray for wear and want of washing, but all with picturesque turrets holding up faded balconies, the people going about their everyday business in long gowns and smart vests, pants fashionably tucked below the knees into leather boots.

One thing Rory always liked about this part of Firene was the few street urchins he saw leaning together in alleyways, no doubt coming up with their next scheme to harass the city guards. It had kept the men entertained when he had been in charge; bored soldiers were a dangerous lot. It seemed like he would provide the entertainment today. He picked up his pace again, skulking between several booths and shuffling behind a crowd of women carrying laundry. *Elven faces,* he thought suddenly, *it is so nice to be around Elven faces again.* Even if he disliked a lot about his people, he couldn't ignore the relief he felt to see them again, to be among his own.

At least in this part of the city, Rory thought, people were honest. Some were hungry, some were poor, but all were acknowledged, not like the city proper where the elite ignored any unfortunates that happened to cross their esteemed path. Here, things were still hard, but the people had adapted. They always did. Rory couldn't help smiling as he allowed a small thief with bright eyes and quick hands to pick his pocket, feigning ignorance as the child ran off with no less than three gold coins. He hurried quickly around the next corner, though, not wanting the child to turn around and find him again when he discovered the color of his coin. At least someone would eat well today.

He dodged another three patrols, aware that the search was intensifying as he had trained them. He wondered idly who was in charge of the army now, then dismissed the thought as he flattened himself against the side of a shop. It didn't matter. Something brushed his arm, and he looked down to see the same face of the young pickpocket next to him, a hand across his lips. The child winked at him, then took a few steps deeper into the alley, bright eyes glowing in the dim light, black hair tucked behind a dirty ear. Rory prepared to slip back out into the street, but the boy grabbed his arm again, "This way," he whispered. "It's safer." Rory considered the odds of ducking patrols for the rest of the way to Caganasti's shop and accepted the urchin's offer.

"Safer?" he asked, taking in the crooked walls lining this alleyway. It was possible the urchin was leading him into a trap, of course.

The boy skidded to a halt abruptly, Rory nearly bumping into him. "Quiet!" the boy demanded, his reasoning becoming clear as the brigade of troops marched by on a street nearby. When they were alone again, the kid squinted at him. "Are you really who they say you are?"

Rory nodded, wondering if he should be flattered. "I am."

"So you're here to claim the throne and change things?" Rory restrained the chuckle that tried to escape his throat. For a child who must have been on the streets for some time, judging by the skill of his fingers, the kid still had some penchant for big dreams. Rory was almost sorry to puncture them.

"No." When the kid continued staring at him, he added, "I'm here to see a friend."

"What friend?" The voice was young and not yet broken, but Rory could hear the sound of a bargainer when he heard it.

Rory considered, calculating the distance and the number of main streets between where he stood and Caganasti. He wouldn't make it without help, not now that the alarm had been sounded, not without wasting a great deal of time, time that Hannah might not have to spare. He gave the kid an appraising look, then decided. "Caganasti," he said. "You know him?"

The urchin nodded, a grin breaking out. "Everyone knows Caganasti. They won't look for you in his shop."

"That's what I'm hoping for." Rory paused, wondering how far he could trust this runt. He was hoping quite a bit. After all, what choice did he have? Not much if he didn't want to end up killing more friends. "Can you get me there?"

"What's in it for me?" the kid retorted.

"Wasn't the gold enough?" Rory asked. At the surprised expression on the boy's face, he added, "You're good, kid, but not that good."

"Two gold," the boy demanded.

"Done," Rory said, handing over the coins without fanfare. The boy bit both coins to check their validity, then shook his head in amazement. "When are you coming back to claim the throne?" he asked. "That will be a great day for this place."

"No more talking," Rory commanded. The boy frowned, nodded, and motioned for Rory to follow again, leading him to a side door in one of the buildings. Once inside, he made his way to a storage closet behind the kitchen and lifted a trap door in the floor. Rory followed the boy down, realizing that he had just discovered an entry into the fabled understreets of Firene. What he wouldn't have given to have known this information a hundred years ago when urchins like this boy had been his daily problem. He could have run drills down in the tunnels, kept the men limber.

The boy seemed to know where he was going, ducking this way and that through the dim corridors, and Rory followed. He wondered if this system of tunnels ran beneath the entire city and had to assume it probably did. Could he use these tunnels to escape after Caganasti found Hannah?

Soon enough, they came to another set of stairs, and Rory found himself exiting a building just across the street from Caganasti's shop. He turned to thank his guide, but the boy had disappeared along with another of his gold pieces. Rory smiled.

Good kid.

Rory approached the crooked porch of Caganasti's shop, the only building with a great deal of gray and not a lot of delicate architecture, carefully scanning the street for more patrols. Caganasti had always preferred utility to aesthetics, and his shop showed his tastes. Unable to hide his relief, Rory pushed the door open cautiously, knowing that anything might lie within.

He let his eyes adjust to the dimness, then entered, stepping carefully on the worn floorboards.

"Caganasti?" he asked, dodging deftly out of the way as a crossbow bolt came streaming toward him. The silver missile buried itself in the door, causing it to shut with a thud, and Rory tugged down his hood to free his head, eyes darting in every direction to see the next shot, if it came.

"Who is it?" asked an angry voice. Rory peeked around a rack of strong-smelling herbs to see a figure hunched low over the counter in the back of the shop. "What the hell do you want?"

"I need a dreamwalker," Rory said, trying not to breathe in the pungent odors as he loosened his weapons, just in case.

"Well, too bad for you. We're fresh out of those here." Another bolt flew toward the door, and Rory listened for the whirring of a crossbow being reloaded. When he heard the tell-tale noise of an undefended foe, he dove across the aisle, coming to a crouch in front of another shelf of odd-shaped boxes.

As Rory hovered, waiting for his opponent's next move, his gaze landed on one of the bigger boxes on the lower shelf. There was a face painted on the surface, a beautiful Elven lady with long blonde hair and sultry eyes; as Rory watched, intrigued, the figure shifted, the eyes winking seductively at him. When nothing rose but his eyebrows, the woman scowled, then the picture faded, replaced by something else. Rory felt an uncontrollable urge to touch the box, to run his fingers across the smooth surface. As he stared, paralyzed, a face began to swim out of the painting, a familiar face with red curls and green eyes, and at the last minute, a blood stain on her chin.

Rory looked away from the picture of Hannah as he had seen her that night with the healer, aware that although he had always known Caganasti's shop held many wonders, djinni women in boxes were not something he had anticipated. He turned his attention back to the store, listening for Caganasti's voice. *Was Caganatsi always so welcoming?* He couldn't recall.

His gaze lighted on a small, blue, glass blown pipe, and he grinned, picking up the delicate object with great care. "That's a shame," he replied, "since you seem to have so many interesting items for sale."

"I don't need your business today," the voice grated. "I'm busy. Get the hell out of my shop."

"Really?" Rory asked, rising to stand and stretching the hand with the pipe lying on the palm out into the no man's land of the main aisle. "So you wouldn't mind if I just drop this then, would you?"

He heard the sharp intake of breath, the sound of Caganasti adjusting his robes and focusing on his newest customer. "Fine," the elf sneered from the dimness. "Come over here. Just don't break it."

"Done," Rory said, stepping out from behind the shelter of the shelves and taking measured steps toward the counter in back. It was an old routine, a ritual test that Caganasti used on anyone who came into his shop. Though Rory didn't remember it being quite so deadly, he assumed that changing times and annoying customers without a shopping agenda might have upped the odds a bit. It was an effective policy all the same—only the very determined ever made it all the way into Caganasti's shop.

The elf hadn't changed much, Rory noted as he set the pipe down on the wooden counter, taking in the wild tangles of black hair tugged through a high topknot, the silver pins slid through the skin of Caganasti's forearms glinting as the elf snatched the pipe and set it deftly beneath the counter, the black ink markings of the fellow's devotion running over patches of bare scalp and down into an inquisitive face. A face that first looked at him impatiently, then squinted, then altered altogether.

"By Horn's fetlock, I never thought you'd make it back here, you old scoundrel!" the elf exclaimed. He hurried out from behind the counter, silver appendages jingling, brushing stray hairs back into one topknot of dreadlocks that were only half as startling as the tattoos that covered every inch of his skin.

"Hello, Caganasti."

"What the hell are you doing back here?" The elf took a brief glance around the shop and at the door. "Are you crazy? Got a death wish? How did you get past the guards? Or are you the one they're all looking for? Never mind." Shaking his head, Caganasti put a hand on Rory's shoulder. "What do you need?" Rory smiled, the mage's unending line of questions a familiar sound.

Rory put an arm around the elf's shoulders, leading him around the counter toward the back room. "I need a favor, old friend."

Caganasti paused, shrugging out from under Rory's gesture of friendship, and stared at him. "That's not all you need. You shouldn't have come back. They won't let you go again."

"I'm not back," Rory said. "In fact, I was never here."

The mage nodded. "Of course, of course, but still... Things have changed, you know, things have changed a great deal."

"Things always change." When the mage seemed about to tell him about all the wonderful changes, Rory spoke quickly. "It's not my concern."

Caganasti narrowed his eyes, one hand stroking his chin. "Then why have you come back?"

"Like I said, I need a dreamwalker."

Caganasti bowed, an elaborate gesture out of place with his exotic demeanor. "At your service, my lord."

"Don't call me that."

"Fine. Tallerin, at least."

"Ha," Rory said, without mirth. "I need you to help me find someone."

Caganasti gestured to the front door, still shut with two bolts in the wooden surface, and a series of clicks signaled the closing of his shop for the day. He motioned to the back room.

"And who are we looking for today? Someone dead, I hope?"

III

THE RIVER

This story takes place between Klauden's Ring and Solyn's Body as Hannah and Rory travel south, adjusting to the limits of her new body.

"Remind me why we are doing this again?" Hannah asked, hunkering on one knee and rubbing her barked shin. She glared at the responsible rock, then transferred the glare to her husband.

The elf stared down at her, face impassive. "Is it bad?" Rory jerked his head at her shin.

Hannah wiped the blood away and flipped the bottom of her dress down, hiding the scrape from his view as she got to her feet. She stared at the blood smeared on her fingers, the sheen glistening in the morning sunlight, saw Rory trying to see how much blood there was, and wiped it quickly on her dress.

Blood was insidious now, an echo of her previous life as a vampire, and an unwelcome reminder of her very brief lifespan now compared to Rory who would live the hundreds of years allotted to elves. In her old body, Hannah would have outlived him. Born vampires like she had been aged so slowly; they could live close to a thousand years if they were smart about it. Fledglings, turned vampires, could potentially live forever—they never changed, bodies frozen in the place when they had been changed.

Now she was neither.

"Hannah?" Rory asked, and he stepped back, coming toward her, no doubt meaning to inspect the cut.

"I'm fine," she said in a low voice that bordered on sharpness, trying to remind herself that he meant well, that his concern was for her well-being because he loved her and wanted her to stay healthy, but sometimes, it didn't feel like that. It felt patronizing. Honestly, did he think her an idiot? Just because she had only spent a few weeks in this human body didn't mean she hadn't learned to respect its fragility.

She had spent her life feeding on humans; she knew how easily they could be broken. Even without her vampiric senses, she was still smart enough to take care of herself. Her body may be new, but she was not.

"Are you sure?" he asked, and she glared at him again.

"I said it's fine."

The elf returned her glare. "Fine," he snapped. "Let's keep going." He started up the path at a brisk trot, and Hannah took advantage of her new body's longer legs to keep pace with him. There were certainly some benefits to this new form. Though she didn't know if she would have chosen to live in a human body, it certainly was better than the alternative—the afterlife was not something Hannah was eager to explore just yet.

There were too many other titillating mortal delights to discover.

And she would enjoy them, she decided, just as soon as they reached the top of this damn mountain, dropped off the package Rory had received in town, picked up anything the old widow wanted brought back down, and collected their pay for this little side jaunt.

They needed the money if they were going to continue south this way. It wasn't that they didn't have money—Rory had plenty of gold in his bag—but gold drew attention, the kind of attention they were trying to avoid, and when the man at the inn mentioned this small favor he needed, it seemed simple enough. In exchange for a quick run up the mountain, an easy morning's travel to the top at the most, they would get three days of bed and board, plus a small fee in copper, coin that was much more common in these smaller villages.

Hannah didn't think anyone from her father's castle was hunting them now, but it was better to be smart as they disappeared. They were conspicuous as it was, the elf and his human female, and people talked about them wherever they went—though mostly about Rory. Apparently, they didn't get a lot of elves in the middle country near the Rasani Mountains. They were well off the beaten path, venturing into geography Hannah had only seen hinted at on old maps. Here in these small towns, even Hannah's blonde hair and pale skin garnered a few looks and whispers. The women here were dark haired and darker skinned, though not as dark as those who lived beyond the far southern desert. Hannah wondered what the people would look like when she and Rory finally stopped moving, when they would find a town and settle there.

Hannah pondered what that life would be like. Though he was her husband now, Rory had only ever been her road companion. They had never stayed in one place for longer than a few nights. She wondered what it would be like to live with Rory in one place, in a small home with a roof and a bed and just the two of them all the time. Hannah wondered what he would do in a town, what they would both do.

She had some skill as a blacksmith, recalled from her last body, though she would likely have to train this body's hands to go through the motions. And she would have to pay closer attention to her work. There had been times when, as a vampire, she had smashed her hand to a pulpy mess in a moment of inattention; then, the solution had been as simple as a fresh infusion of blood. Now, such an incident would cripple her for life. The idea still galled her sometimes.

She stared at Rory's back, watching the elf as he walked along the mountain path, shoulders straight and feet sure as they picked their way among the rocks. His arms swung loosely at his sides, arms that held her close to him at night with hands that pressed against her in ways that made all of the minor inconveniences of this fragile mortal body worthwhile. There was the blood, of course, or lack thereof. She could kiss him and hold him and just hear his heartbeat echoing when she lay on his chest—not feel the pull of his pulse calling to her from across the room, demanding that she taste him. It was oddly freeing to not want him like that anymore.

And it made everything worth it.

She took a deep breath, something she thought she would never get tired of doing, relishing the feel of her chest filling with air, her breasts pressing against the front of her dress, and closed her eyes to truly appreciate the exhale. As a vampire, she could breathe if she wanted to, but she hadn't needed to. The relief from such a simple act in this human body was overwhelming; she was still savoring the feeling.

And then her foot caught on something, and by the time she opened her eyes, she was already tumbling off the path, hitting a tree, and then sliding right off the edge of the mountain, slow mortal reflexes not nearly enough to catch her.

She heard Rory call her name, but then she was falling. She hit the ground hard on her upper back, remaining air pushed out of her lungs, and she gagged as her body continued to move, feet flopping over her head as she continued down, body picking up dirt and rocks as she rolled, feet occasionally bouncing off trees as she pinged from one obstacle to the next. She tried to reach out to grab something, anything, managed to snag a tree limb that slowed her for a second, and then the rest of her body slid sideways and out over more empty air. She heard a disheartening crack from the branch she held, and then it let go, and she was falling, really falling now. She managed to look around as a shelf of rock rushed past her on one side, and then she hit the water, body slamming into the frigid river like a solid wall.

She came to the surface in a sputter, all of her limbs flailing, nearly overcome with panicked thoughts. *I can't swim, and now I'm going to drown! This body was the worst idea ever! Damn Klauden for putting me into it!*

Thoughts of her old friend calmed her, and she suddenly heard his voice in her head, the calm historian, soothing and patient. *Focus, chaivin. Take stock of the situation.*

She continued her frantic paddling, feet kicking uselessly into more water as she tried to look around. She was in the middle of a river, water spreading out on both sides to banks of rocky edges and mud-crusted trees. The water was moving fast, the current dragging her along in its wake, her clothing heavy and trying to pull her under. She focused on her feet first, using one foot to push the boot off of the other, and was relieved when she bobbed to the surface, one boot no longer weighing her down. She used her bare foot to shove her other boot free, and then she was floating more easily, her hair a tangle in her face as she tried to find a way out. She had to swim or try something better than this flailing in order to get to the edge, but which side?

She tried to find the horizon, the thin line of the setting sun a guide in the rush of water, and putting her back to it, she knew that Rory should be on her right side. She started kicking that way, moving with the current as best she could but trying to gain a few precious feet closer to the edge. The bank whooshed by, sometimes a rock shelf, sometimes a muddy swath, and she pressed her feet down, seeking the bottom. Her dress tangled around her legs, bunched up at her middle, then pulled down again, tugging her with it. She sputtered, gasping for breath before she went under and pumping with her arms to reach the surface again. Her heart was pounding, the sound echoing in her head under the water.

She became aware of another sound then, a roaring that went beyond her panic and the all too human blood rushing through her veins.

She kicked, face breaking the surface, and the roaring got louder.

Oh no.

Hannah knew that sound. When they approached the mountain, she and Rory had paused to admire the waterfalls, standing at the bottom and refilling their waterskins, taking their time as they soaked in the natural majesty of so much water falling from the top of the mountain.

It had been pretty.

Now, she was stuck in the flow of the river, fast approaching the cliff that formed the waterfall. Hannah cursed. She could see where the river ended up ahead. She could also make out what might be rocks rising out of the middle of the water. Hannah started flailing back toward the middle, aiming for the rocks.

It was a small chance, but she'd take it.

Hannah spread her arms and legs wide, hoping to hit the rocks with at least some part of her body. The force of impact was enough to make her vision dance at the edges, and the water flung her sideways. Hannah held on to the edge, digging her fingers into the rock like claws as the rest of her body swung outward with the thrust of the water. Her weight pushed her down, and then she was dangling from the edge of a cliff, water roaring around her on both sides as she held onto rough edges above. She tried to pull herself up, but her arms were exhausted from fighting the water. She quickly gave that up, focusing on other options. She peered down, trying to see what lay beneath her. There was water, yes, and fog from the spray, but she was pretty sure that there was an outcropping of rock far below her. Her fingers were screaming in protest, her fingernails pulling as she gripped the rock. She had to let go.

I will fall, she thought clearly, and on the heels of that, *and that's alright*.

She conjured the words to the spell with a desperation she didn't know she had in her, spewed them forth just as her fingers let go, and then she was falling, but softly, gently, the magic allowing her to float until her feet touched down on a small outcropping of rock far below. She let the magic help her to her knees, then fell forward, aching hands held tight to her chest, and curled up. She lay on her side for a moment, just breathing. When she opened her eyes, she saw that the slab of rock she now occupied was actually the entrance to a cave. She scooted farther into the darkness, away from the biting cold of the water spray, and curled up once more.

She just needed to sleep for a moment. After that, she could take stock.

A small voice deep inside her head cried out at this thought, but Hannah only understood the very last word. "Light."

Yes, she thought dazedly, as the darkness enveloped her, *light would be nice*.

She knew the words, mumbled them through numb lips, but by the time the spell blazed forth, she was already unconscious.

Rory heard the sound of Hannah stumbling, her boot dragging against something on the ground. He turned around as she made a surprised sound, and he saw her tilt dangerously to the edge of the path. He reached for her, her sleeve grazing him as she tumbled, and then she was beyond his reach. He watched in horror as she first slammed into a tree, skidded to the side, then twisted over the edge and dropped out of sight. He was moving at once, hands grasping for tree limbs to steady himself as he followed her path, holding tight to a final tree as he leaned forward to see over the edge.

He heard a thump and more noise, and the hand that had been squeezing his chest released a fraction. At least she hadn't fallen very far. Listening to the sound of Hannah's jolting trip down the mountain though, he wondered if it would matter. He could make out the motion of her tumbling form below him, sliding from tree to tree, hitting, he was pretty certain, every single one on the way by, and he saw that she was fast approaching yet another edge.

Damn the luck!

He couldn't see where that one led from his perch up here, so he gave a quick prayer to the gods and let go of the tree, trusting his instincts to help him keep his feet. He landed solidly, but the soft dirt quickly gave way beneath his boots. He was ready for that though, leaping deftly down the incline from rocks to the base of trees, this time stepping lightly on a stump, there bouncing quickly off of a mound of twisted roots. He saw Hannah's bag, abandoned against a flattened bush, and snagged it as he ran past. He was making good time, halfway to the drop-off when he watched Hannah go over the side.

He listened for the sound of her landing for far too long, his own heart pounding in his ears along with the same litany of *No! No! No!* in his mind, and then there was a splash. Rory's heart sank further than he thought possible. He ran the last few paces to the edge, catching himself on a tree limb as he slid to a stop before going over. He looked out into the empty space, then down, far down, to the rushing water below.

Hannah had fallen into the damn river. He really should have taken the time to teach her to swim before now. It hadn't seemed like an important thing; they could swim when they reached the place they decided to settle in. Besides, the water was still way too cold for any fun. A few more weeks and farther travel to the south would make the lessons far more enjoyable. Clearly, he had been a fool to wait. He should have known Hannah would need to learn as soon as possible. She was always getting herself into ridiculous situations.

He scanned the cliff he stood on, hands quickly pulling at vines and roots, judging his path down to the river's edge. He could see that the cliff dipped in underneath him, but he was fairly certain he could climb down if luck was with him. He knelt at the edge, let Hannah's bag hang below him for a second, then dropped it, not waiting to see if it landed on the edge and missed the water. He grabbed hold of the nearest root and started over the edge, confident hands finding grips along the way. There was a moment when he reached the underside of the cliff and thought this was probably a bad idea, especially when the root in his hand sprang free with a twang and left him dangling from one hand. But then his feet swayed to the rock wall, finding purchase among the nooks and crannies there, and soon he was skidding and sliding his way to the ground below.

He saw Hannah's bag in the mud near the edge of the water, scooped it up, and began hurrying down along the river, scanning the surface for Hannah. Was she able to stay afloat? Or had the fall knocked her unconscious and was she, even now, drowning under the surface?

Rory forced himself to calm down, feet sure on the ground as he moved, eyes scanning from side to side. He caught motion far ahead, and he saw a small shape flailing. He doubled his speed again, ears registering what he had been trying not to think about—the roar of the waterfall ahead.

She couldn't swim; he knew that for sure—but maybe she could paddle to the edge and get out of the water in time. Judging by the swift current rushing by as he ran alongside, though, Rory doubted it. He was a strong swimmer, and he didn't know if he would be able to fight the water in this river.

If she had her old strength, sure, she would have been able to get out just fine. Of course, if she were in her old impervious body, neither water nor cliffs nor any amount of bodily harm—save fire—would have been able to stop her. Now, though, she was human. Fragile.

Part of him knew it was better this way since now they could actually be together without her turning him into a fledgling, but at the moment, he'd give anything for Hannah's old body.

He kept his eyes on that bobbing form, feet finding purchase on rocks and fallen trees and mud as he followed. He was almost near her when she bounced into the rock at the edge, and he saw her slide slowly over the edge. He yelled in frustration, then slid along the edge, trying to get a better view of the falls from the side. He couldn't see the water at the bottom through the mist, but he didn't actually see Hannah fall down there. Maybe she was holding on somehow?

He picked his way carefully along the rocks that marked the cliff's edge to a tree that hung out over the opening. He dropped Hannah's bag, using both hands to shimmy out on a limb in order to see more of the falls. Through the misty water haze, he saw a small form dangling from the cliff in the middle of the falls. As he watched, the hands let go, but instead of plummeting into the water, Hannah dropped slowly, the glow of magic surrounding her entire body. She landed on a small outcropping of rock, then collapsed on the ground. Rory was certain for a terrifying moment that she was dead, the spell some kind of contingency magic designed to take care of her body in the event of her death. But then the body moved, slumped to one side, and slid forward on the shelf, away from the water and the edge. Another glow surrounded her, and Rory recognized her light spell. She didn't move again, but the light illuminated the opening of a cave beyond where she lay.

If he could get to her, he could help her. He might not have Klauden's gift of healing magic, but he knew how to bind wounds, knew how to keep people alive, and he could do that. Hannah was alive. It was enough.

He just had to get to her.

Judging the distance, Rory knew he couldn't jump from here, and the water was too swift for him to swim across from the edge. He could try, but he didn't think it was possible. He could try swimming from farther upstream, but even then, in such a strong current, he wasn't sure he could hit the mark perfectly. More likely, he'd go sailing off the edge with the water—and he didn't have a soft fall spell to ease his landing.

He looked at the rock below him, the cliff walls, debating if he could climb down somehow. He would have to go behind the waterfall to reach the ledge where Hannah lay, and he didn't think he could hold on with so much water pouring down on him.

Calculating, he considered the edge of the tree limb on which he lay.

He had rope. He could tie it to the edge of this tree, climb down, and swing himself over there. He had read stories as a child of the great jungle elves who swung on vines from tree to tree. It was crazy, but he had to try. His hands were strong. He could hold on. And the tree was sturdy enough.

It was the only plan he had.

It took him a few moments to shimmy back to the edge, secure his belongings and Hannah's bag tightly to his body, then climb back out on the tree, rope in hand. He tied a knot around the tree limb he lay on, then added a sturdy loop at the bottom of the rope and knots every few feet. His grip was good, his hands strong, but the rope would be wet. He would slide all over the place as soon as he reached the water.

Saying a quick prayer to whatever gods would listen, Rory slipped off the limb down onto the rope, feet gaining solid purchase on the knots as he moved to the bottom. When he was about level with the ledge Hannah lay on, he started to sway, kicking his body back and forth to gain enough momentum to cross the gap between him and the ledge. The water hurt when he swung into it, but he got enough range of motion to actually kick off the cliff under the tree, propelling himself through the spray and onto the ledge. He wanted to hold on to the rope—it was their only certain escape route—but it wasn't long enough, and he could feel it trying to pull him back out over empty space. He let go, falling in a heap on the ledge behind Hannah, one foot sliding back over empty air before he fell forward on top of her. His weight on her caused her to gasp, a loud "oof!" that reassured him. If she could make a sound like that, she was still alive.

If she was still alive, everything would be alright.

Hannah woke to someone touching her face. The feeling was warm, a soothing contrast to the cold numbness she felt everywhere else. She thought her body might start to hurt soon, the emptiness a promise of pain to come, but for now, she lay still, relishing the warmth bathing her face.

She opened her eyes, and Rory was looking down at her, a cloth in his hand as he wiped her cheek. A relieved smile spread across his face as he saw she was awake, breaking through the mask of worry. Hannah had a moment of complete dislocation—she had been here before, lying on her back as Rory wiped her face, and she had been wounded then, aching with bloodfever—but that had been months ago, in another body, next to a different river. Rory hadn't yet known what she was then.

Movement at her side brought her back to the present. Glancing down, she saw that Rory was holding one of her hands gently in his, her fingers resting on his palm. Her fingers were numb, but she could see that they were a reddish purple, and her fingernails were ragged, some nails lifted from her fingers, and one nail torn off her ring finger. That was really going to hurt when she could feel again.

She noticed that she could actually see and looked around for the light source. She was lying on her back in a small cave, a hastily built fire burned brightly against the wall near her feet, pouring smoke from damp twigs and leaves, and she realized the roar she had thought was inside her head was actually the sound of the waterfall outside. She looked at the opening of the cave and the ledge beyond. A small amount of late afternoon light peeked in around the water.

"What ... happened?" she managed to say through cracked lips.

"What do you remember?" he asked softly, laying her hand down on her chest and pushing her hair out of her face and behind her ears, fingers resting against the line of her jaw.

"I tripped," she said and laughed, the sound choked as it came out. Rory cupped her cheek, holding her as she coughed. "I'm pretty sure I hit every single tree on the way down."

Rory laughed then too, tension going out of him as he released her. "I thought the same thing!"

"Well," she said, "if I'm going to fall off a mountain, I suppose I should do it right."

"Oh Hannah," he breathed, and he was near her again, body cradling hers as she giggled helplessly. Feeling was creeping back into her hands, her fingers singing with fire, and she moaned a little.

"Here," Rory said, producing a small glass bottle from his bag. "I didn't want to give it to you until you woke up, but it will take away some of the pain."

Hannah sat up a bit in his arms and allowed him to tip the bottle into her mouth. She took a few small sips of the bitter liquid, coughed, and then lay back down. Rory stared at her. She could feel him taking stock of her injuries and waited for the inevitable anger at her clumsiness. Though she could see the worried frustration in him, he didn't say anything, instead watching her silently.

"How bad am I?" Hannah whispered, feeling the liquid steal through her limbs, pain vanishing in a haze of warm drowsiness.

He shook his head, eyes closing as he took a deep breath. "Not bad, considering," Rory replied, looking at her again, his face unreadable. "Your hands are actually the worst of it. You have some bruises and scrapes on your arms, legs, and back, but you should recover. You are very lucky to be alive." He paused, hands rubbing her shoulders through the damp material of her dress. "You're so cold, Hannah. Let's get you out of those wet clothes."

Hannah mumbled something in response, but then she was dreaming of warmth and quiet.

The next time she opened her eyes, the fire had burned down to a low glow. Rory's metal lantern sat near her head, a small pinprick of light in the dimness of the cave. She was curled up against Rory, their bare skin pressed against each other, his cloak serving as a blanket for them both. Hannah wondered how long she had been naked, and she spied her dress spread out next to the small fire, presumably drying. Rory's clothes were also laid out, and she ran a hand along the smooth planes of his chest and hips. Her fingers hurt, but it was distant still. In the light of the lantern, she could see that the redness of cold had vanished, replaced by some dark purple that would likely bruise. Her fingernails were a disaster, though she could see that Rory must have trimmed the worst edges while she was out. She could see the raw exposed flesh from under her nails, but nothing was bleeding, so that was a good sign. She tried to flex her fingers, felt the skin tight at her knuckles and the pain sharp, but not unbearable.

Looking down at herself, she saw that she had a few darkening bruises on her ribs and arms, and her face ached like she may have a black eye, but Rory had been right. Her hands had taken the worst of it.

She had been so incredibly lucky.

She was still marveling at divine blessings when Rory stirred under her, eyes opening lazily to look down at her.

"Hey," he said, arm coming around her back to pull her close, but gently, mindful of her bruises.

"Hey," she replied.

"How..." He paused, not wanting to finish the question. She could feel the tension in him as he pushed some strong emotion aside. Instead, he looked around the small cave. "It's not bad, you know."

Hannah cocked an eyebrow. "What isn't bad?"

"Well, all things considered, this is quite cozy. Fire, waterfall, small cave, all alone in the wilderness with the woman I love..."

Hannah tapped him playfully on the arm with the palm of her hand, careful not to touch anything with her fingers. "Trapped in a tiny cave behind a waterfall after nearly falling to my death... yeah, definitely cozy."

His hand started rubbing her shoulder, and then her neck, long fingers pressing delightfully into all of her favorite places. She gave him a look. "Seriously?"

He grinned. "It's not like we have anywhere else to be right now. And you seem to be feeling fine."

"My hands aren't so fine," she commented, pressing close to him, but careful of where her fingers were.

"No, they will take a bit to heal." He pressed his hand against hers softly, her hand small in his but not as small as she had been. "But you will recover," he paused, then added, "and I am thankful for it."

She quirked an eyebrow at him, pulling away a little bit to see more of him. "What do you mean: thankful? I'm hurt. I'm lucky I didn't die today."

"I know," he replied and kissed her. When he stopped, he whispered, "Wounds remind you that you are still alive, and that is always a good thing."

"Always?" she murmured, the warmth of him so close and tempting.

"Always," he replied, and then there was no more talking for a time.

In the morning, Hannah sat quietly while Rory slept, carefully flipping pages in her spellbook with aching thumbs and forefingers. She finally let the book fall closed, words of the spell solidifying in her mind, and sighed. It would be enough, she decided, reaching for her bag, mindful not to let any stray water splash the magic book. She knew it would survive just about anything, but she was still careful, and she slid it gently back into her bag with reverence. Rory was restless when he woke, getting dressed quickly, and immediately scanning their surroundings in the morning light. She joined Rory where he stood at the edge, peering down into the mist below.

She glanced from where they stood to the tree that grew out over the cliffs, the rope still dangling from it, slowly drifting in the breeze. "You really swung across the chasm on a rope?" she asked again, marveling at the elf she had married. "I really wish I could have seen that!"

"It was a damn foolish thing to do," he admitted, "but I couldn't think of another way to get to you." The tension in him was back, and she tried to ignore it.

Hannah stepped close to the edge of the ledge, leaning over to peer into the depths. Rory's hand grabbed her shoulder and pushed her back, and she repressed the urge to snap at him. *Does he really think I'm going to fall off the edge?*

"We could jump," she said, if only to see his horrified reaction. He saw she was joking and shook his head with a sigh of frustration.

"We could try to climb back up or maybe swing over to the side somehow," Rory offered, then looked at her hands, face darkening at the sight of her raw flesh. "But you're not climbing anything like that. You can't even hold on to anything."

Hannah pursed her lips, considering. Rory moved beside her and suddenly pulled her close, kissing her soundly as he tugged her away from the edge. "Maybe we could just stay here for a few more days until you heal up."

She pushed him away. "Cute," she said, but she saw how he looked at her face in the morning light, guessing that she must be bruised badly on her face. He was buzzing a bit at the edges, clearly angry but trying not to say anything, distracting himself by kissing her instead. He wasn't getting out of this so easily. She pressed her hands to his chest, pushing him back against the cliff wall to the side of the cave opening. "Out with it," she demanded. "What is going on?"

He stared at her, face blank. "I don't know what you mean."

"Like hell," she snarled. "You're pissed at something. What?"

His face broke, and the frustration showed through. He gestured at their surroundings. "This, okay? I'm a little bit annoyed at this ... situation."

Hannah followed his gesture. "What? Being stuck here? Last night, you were talking about how cozy everything is."

He glared at her. "Look, Hannah. I'm glad you're alive. I am. Truly." He looked around again, then back at her. "But I wish you'd be more careful so we wouldn't find ourselves in these kinds of situations."

There. He had said it.

Hannah felt the heat rise in her face, the bruised area around her eyes throbbing in time to her heartbeat. If she were still a vampire, she would have sensed the blood rising inside. She could see a matching red glow creeping up Rory's neck.

"Do you honestly think I fell off a mountain on purpose?" she asked, voice quietly menacing.

"No. But I do think that you need to pay more attention to things. You should be dead!

The only reason you're not is because you were damned lucky. And your magic—" He stopped abruptly, staring at her, some realization hitting him hard.

She nodded at him, gloating a little as she watched him finally get it. "Yes," she said. "My magic."

He looked around again, then back at her. "Can you get us out of here?"

She nodded. "Of course. What do you think I was doing all morning while you slept?"

He ignored the barb. "Then let's go," he said, pushing past her to collect his bag. Hannah stood where she was.

"No."

"No?" He turned to face her, face questioning.

She shook her head. "We're not finished here."

Rory looked up to the water above them. "We should have reached that widow yesterday. She'll be waiting on us now."

"And she can wait," Hannah said flatly.

"For what?"

"For you to apologize for being a pompous ass."

Rory stared at her, red creeping across both cheeks, chest moving a little as he took deep breaths. "And how have I been an ass?" he asked quietly.

"Look at you, so angry at me because I tripped and fell."

"You are constantly tripping and falling," he reminded her sharply. "You run around in that body like it's your old one, and you're going to get yourself killed! I'm an ass for worrying about you?"

"No, you're an ass because you don't trust me." She closed the gap between them, hands pressing against his face and cupping his cheeks. "I know this body is fragile. I'm learning to take care of it. I could do that a lot better if you stopped babying me."

"Babying you? Hannah, you fell off the mountain because you weren't paying attention!"

"Yes, and I survived!"

"You survived because you were incredibly lucky!"

"I survived because I was lucky—but also because of my magic. I am not helpless, Rory. I am not this girl." She gestured at her body. "I'm still *me* in here. You don't seem to remember that."

"I see you," he insisted.

"Do you? Because it *just* occurred to you that I could use my magic to get us out of here. In my old body, you wouldn't have doubted it for a minute. You would rely on me. But now, you just see her—this clumsy, tall human who trips and falls and hurts herself."

"I just don't want to lose you."

"And I appreciate that, but right now, you're barely seeing me at all." Hannah moved away from him to the other side of the ledge. She could feel the spray of the water on her face, cool against the heat under her skin, but she ignored it.

Rory seemed about to say something, then stopped himself, staring hard at her instead. When he did speak, his voice was calm, considering. "When I saw you go over the edge yesterday, I thought you were dead." He paused, chest hitching a little. "And I never want to feel that way again." Hannah tried to imagine what that might feel like, watching Rory disappear over the edge of a cliff, and she waited for him to continue. His face was red, eyes dark with remembered emotion. "But then I saw you hanging on to the edge, and when you fell that time, I was sure, sure you were gone." He shook his head then, a small grin replacing the fear. "Then I saw the magic, and for a moment, I thought it was a contingency, like Malbrek used, a spell designed to go off in the event of your death. But it wasn't anything like that." He stepped over to her.

"You used your magic," he said, a hint of pride in his voice now. "Disoriented, wounded, and dangling from a waterfall, you used your magic to save yourself."

Hannah nodded, wanting to make a dismissive sound. *Why wouldn't I use my magic to save myself?* But she waited for him to continue. "I know you, Hannah. Not this body, but you. Truly."

Hannah smirked at him. "You say that now, sure, but what about the next time something happens? Will you depend on me, or will you rush to defend me from myself?"

He didn't answer right away. Hannah waited, giving him time and space to think about it. "I will ... try," he said eventually.

"Okay," she said, accepting his words at face value. "That's all I ask."

"But if you insist on throwing yourself off cliffs, I am going to pester you about taking better care of yourself," he added.

"Agreed," she said, reaching out a hand to him. He took hers gently, letting her fingers rest on his palm. "Now hold on to me. I'm going to get us out of here."

Rory reached out to grab both of her shoulders, and she recited the spell carefully, allowing the magic to pour out of her. The levitation spell wasn't something she did often, and it required a great deal of concentration and power to lift both of them, but she managed to slowly raise them off the ledge, up above the waterfall, above the river, over the mountain edge, and back to the path. Hannah watched the awe-struck admiration on Rory's face as they moved through the air, smiling at the sheer joy on his face as they sank back down to the ground. Hannah could see the spot a few feet ahead where she had originally stumbled. There was a root lying in the path, a small thing really, but enough to trip an unsuspecting foot. She waited for her head to clear from the magic, felt the low thrum in her temples that signaled an impending headache, and took Rory's hand, leading him up the path, careful to step over the root this time.

Rory stepped up next to her, keeping pace easily, but he wasn't watching her every move, and Hannah felt a small surge of hope. Maybe he really would stop worrying about her all the time.

The combination of magic and wounds caught up to her before they reached the widow's house, and Hannah paused. She took a drink of water from her waterskin, a hand to her forehead. She was wounded, and the spell had been a big one. She really wanted to sleep in a bed as soon as possible.

Rory looked at her, but he didn't say anything.

"I could use a drink," she admitted. "Even some of that whiskey you have. It's awful stuff, but it would be nice right about now." She paused, feeling the shrieking pain of her body, this terribly weak body. "Or maybe just a good knife to put me out of my misery."

Rory grinned at her, hands at his belt. "I'm pretty sure I have a blade handy," he replied. "Would you prefer a stiletto or the longsword?"

"I don't know," she answered. "Would you trust me with either while walking on this path?"

Her husband smiled at her. "I trust you, Hannah. I will always trust you."

IV

OLD FRIENDS AND NEW BUSINESS

*This story takes place at the same time as Klauden's Ring
and features characters who appear in Hannah's Heart.*

C aptain Red surveyed *The Volant* from where she stood on the dock.
Her three-masted caravel looked right at home amid the other ships
visiting the city, not too big or too small among the others spending a few
days in Firene.

The portmaster hurried away, her docking fee clear in one hand and
his stack of official paperwork in the other, his pockets slightly heavier
than they had been before she had walked down from her vessel. Her gaze
moved from her ship, sails neatly stowed and ropes expertly tied, to the
small huddle of houses that lined the shore at the edge of the dock. Firene
was known as the gleaming city of white stone buildings, but down here at
the docks, the houses were wood, some clearly constructed of driftwood
and discarded pieces of old boats.

Some things never change.

She looked up the lane to the city proper. It had been a long time since
she'd first been here, standing on this very dock with all of her belongings
stowed in a pack that was far too expensive to remain long in her possession. Thinking back, Red tried to calculate the years.

She'd been young then, a foolish girl with no notions of how the
world really worked, just knowing that the life her family wanted for her
was not the one she would have. Her first ship had been out of Upsen years

later, but her first time at sea had been stolen away on a ship from this city. She'd run here at first from her family's estate in Ruyan, hiding from her family and their expectations.

A foolish plan, of course. How much easier could it be to find the human in the Elven city?

Firene hadn't truly changed in the years since, and had she stayed in the city as she had intended, they would have found her soon enough. She learned quickly that unlike the city above, the lower ward near the docks was a mixture of all races. The elves may like their city for themselves, but they had no objections to glittering Morovian gems, sumptuous Carisan fabrics, and the wide range of spices that didn't grow this far north; the docks were always bustling with trade from other places.

No one was likely to question her presence if she stayed in the lower city. Travelers often frequented the shops and taverns there. Now, if she were foolish enough to wander into the city proper, as she had when she first arrived, green with inexperience and clouded by the privilege of her blue blood, there would be questions.

Fortunately, her business this time was nearby. Caganasti was no fool; the elf's magic shop was perfectly positioned near the blurry edges between districts—just far enough between the High Street and the lower ward to allow business from either to come inside without comment.

Red assumed his shop would be watched by the guard, but she didn't think it mattered. She hadn't done anything to warrant trouble near Firene. It was too important for her regular trade to risk her good name. They knew her here as Captain Red, the one who got your goods where you wanted them, no problems, no debate, and no questions asked.

And if they also know what they call me down in Upsen, well, no one here is going to say anything as long as I cover the fees and then some.

Even so, she normally sent her first mate into towns to do the ordinary dealing. Lady Black was quite skilled at getting the best price for her work, loyal in a way that could be exploited someday, but a dedicated and reliable companion. Red only oversaw things personally if it was really important or extremely dangerous—or the customer was paying extra for discretion. Jocelyn Black may be a clever negotiator, always on the edge of mendacious, but she was not subtle; people always remembered her ebony skin, her long braids—great for recognition and respect but not always ideal for the situation. If things went well this trip, Red wouldn't have to worry about people recognizing either of them again. She thought of the Book in her bag, suppressed a shudder, and took a few steps away from her ship.

Tucking her tell-tale hair up under her hat, Red made her way down the dock, adjusting her posture as she moved. There was no reason to draw attention to herself if she could avoid it this time. Sometimes her name was the perfect lubricant to ease a business proposal along—but this wasn't one of those times. Caganasti would know her, and that was enough for this visit.

She adjusted the package under her arm, careful to keep the top of the bag upright so nothing spilled out or showed to the curious eye of a bystander. The bag was enchanted to keep her safe from any ill effects, but it wouldn't do to start shooting magic into the street, calling attention to herself. Firene was generally a safe city. Most people weren't willing to risk a run-in with guards who'd had hundreds of years of training, but there might be one who would think a clearly magic spellbook worth the gamble, especially down here in the lower ward where people liked to look the other way.

Red gave her ship one last longing look from the end of the dock, then hunched her shoulders and started moving briskly into the streets, altering her gait to mimic a teenage boy set on business. She let her gaze wander, a youngster set free for a moment eager to soak in the city, but focused enough to get the job done.

No one paid her much attention as she walked through the streets to Caganasti's shop. She planned her strategy as she walked, knowing that the elf had a penchant for traps at the front door. He expected her—the letters had seen to that—but he didn't know that she would arrive today—only that she was eventually coming to trade. Red didn't think it would matter anyway. The old elf had an odd sense of humor.

She was turning off a side street into a main thoroughfare, thoughts focused on her destination, but still scanning her surroundings, when she saw him. Her thoughts froze, and her feet stopped walking. She stood in place, eyes widening as she took in the form of Lord Stefan Grayson. It had been twenty years since she had last seen him in her father's study, but age had been good to him. He was still fit, shoulders wide and waist trim, and his once pale blonde hair had faded to white waves that framed his face. He was well-dressed—no surprise there—but the sigil around his neck had changed. He had been a Lord of his House then, his office signified by the blue gem around his neck, but now he wore the round gold disc of an ambassador beneath his House stone.

Good, Red thought, surveying her would-be paramour from across the street. *Stefan was always a great talker—he would excel at dealings between Houses and cities.*

He is still just as handsome as he was all those years ago.

Red wondered if her father would have chosen Lord Grayson for her in the end if she hadn't run away. She had bristled at the thought of an arranged match, but Stefan was always kind to her, and she had liked him the most out of all of her suitors. If she had been given a choice of them, she might have chosen him.

Of course, her father had no intention of giving her a choice.

Red pulled herself back into the moment, aware that a few people had noticed the tall boy who had stopped dead in the middle of the street. She needed to keep moving. She watched Stefan take a few steps down the street. He hadn't noticed her at all. If she could just move her feet, he likely wouldn't see her at all.

The years have really been good to him. She took in his form around the strands of red hair that had come loose from her hat.

She was just about to start moving again, dismissing old flames and re-focusing on her plan to get around Caganasti's traps, when Stefan turned to survey the street and saw her. His gaze skipped over her, paused, and then came back with an intensity that surprised her. She reached up to her hat, hoping to hide her telltale hair, but she could see it was too late. Stefan was closing the distance between them, his face bright with joy, eyes eager with curiosity.

When he stood a few feet from her, he paused and gave her a perfectly cordial bow. She replied in kind, her body moving without her consent, the distance of two decades forgotten as she looked at him.

"My Lady Serena Rayven," he said, low voice quiet with awe, "as I live and breathe."

She curtsied even though she was wearing pants instead of a dress, unable to stop herself, and her hand reached out automatically. He caught it with practiced grace, warm lips placing a gentle kiss on the back of her hand. "My lord Grayson," she greeted him, foolishly hoping that he wouldn't notice the calluses that now covered her palms, fingers strong from years of working ropes, skin battered from saltwater and sun, "I am surprised that you remember me."

He took in her simple clothing, the brown pants, the white shirt, the leather vest and jacket, but his eyes lingered on the hat and scarf. "You may dress differently, my lady, but you have not changed at all. I would know you anywhere."

Red blushed at this, her mind still trying to wrap itself around this chance encounter. It had been many years since anyone had called her by her true name, since she had shared her old self with anyone, and it felt really good to hear someone say it—to hear *him* say it again.

"You are also looking well," she told him, remembering her manners as she withdrew her hand. "The northern air agrees with you."

He nodded, taking the compliment in stride. "This city is certainly keeping me occupied." He paused, then added, "You are still as lovely as ever." He looked at her more closely, and for a moment, she thought his hand may reach out to touch her face. "What land is it that has kept you so fine?"

Red felt her cheeks warming again and tried to get ahold of herself. This was ridiculous. *I am a woman of eight and thirty—far too old to be blushing on the street like a girl of fifteen!* She couldn't remember the last time she had felt like this. She thought back to her last lover, a young man who had gone his way when they reached Warin. It hadn't been that long ago. *Am I so desperate for a shag that I am reduced to thrills from old acquaintances?*

"Oh," she said, pausing for time, "here and there. I go where the wind takes me these days."

Stefan smiled, and then his face grew serious. "Have you traveled much then, lady?"

Red thought of the land beyond the northern mountains, of the so-called wild men in their wolf pelts who had let her hunt with them, of the tribes she had dealt with in the southern peninsula, of the small whorl of tattooed ink high on her left thigh placed there by Nasuk when she finally earned the People's trust, of people and places far and wide.

"Yes," she told him, face beaming with pride. She was not that girl in her father's study anymore. "I have been many places."

Stefan leaned in again. He seemed to hesitate, but then the words came out as if he couldn't stop them. "Did you never marry, my lady?"

Red shook her head. "No." She paused, then grinned at him. "Did you, my lord?"

Stefan returned her grin. "Oh no. I learned early on that the game of marriage was one I was not quite qualified enough to win." At her expression, he added, "I never did seem to have enough to offer ... beyond my good name, that is."

"It is a good name," she said, and before the moment grew awkward, she continued. "So now you travel as well?" she asked, gesturing to his necklace. "An ambassador to the elves?"

He nodded. "Only for the last few months, scarcely a moment if you ask them, but my Elvish has improved a great deal." He chuckled. "It is not exactly the life I imagined back when I knew you, but it suits me." He paused, then laughed. "Perhaps your father was right after all, my lady. What would I do with a wife and family? I am never in the same place long enough."

Red smiled but couldn't quite bring herself to laugh. She may be standing here free on this street corner now, twenty years beyond her father's reach, but it didn't change what he had done, what might have been. Red wondered if another twenty years would be long enough to admit that her father hadn't always been wrong about everything.

Maybe, but probably not.

Red considered Stefan, at the man she might have married, and though she still liked him, she was glad that her life had gone another way. "Nor the life I imagined," she agreed, but her mind was already skipping away from him, away from what might have been. "And while it has been delightful to see you again, my lord, I must be on my way. I have a prior engagement."

Stefan nodded, stepping away from her as courtesy demanded. "Of course." He hesitated another moment, then added, "Will you be in town long? Where are you staying? I would love to see you again."

Red smiled, but her expression was rueful. "I am only here for the day to meet a friend. Then I'm on my way." She gave her a real smile then, truth filling her face. "It really was wonderful to see you again, my lord."

He smiled in return, but she could see the sadness in his eyes. She considered. *Perhaps I can meet him after my business? What harm can it do to reminisce with an old friend?*

The moment stretched out as she contemplated, but then she stopped herself. She knew what such reminiscing would lead to, and after an evening of fine dining and expensive wine, she would have to explain why she had to leave so soon, no doubt slipping out of his rooms while still tying her laces. Another time, such an encounter would have overruled her sense of urgency. Red looked down at the bag she still held carefully against her side.

Not while she traveled with the damned Book. Red had no magic of her own, but even she could feel the Book tingling with power so close to her. She would be glad when it was away from her. She just hoped that Caganasti had acquired the item she intended to trade it for.

She could have used the amulet to avoid being recognized by Stefan.

Stefan, she mused, how quickly her thoughts had gotten on a first name basis with a man she hadn't seen in decades.

"Then I thank you for the few moments we have shared, my lady," Lord Grayson said, cordiality back on his face like a mask. He bowed again, this time in farewell. "I will not keep you from your errand, though I hope we may run into one another again. Your servant, my lady." He kept his face down, clearly her signal to walk away. Red got her feet to take the first step away from him, then moved more quickly down the street. She risked a quick glance back when she reached the next corner, saw that he had looked up and was watching her go. It was a small break from the rules of interaction, but one she could forgive. They weren't in her father's parlor after all.

She enjoyed knowing that he watched her walk away, no doubt also thinking of missed opportunities. Nevertheless, she turned down the next street even though she didn't need to, wanting to keep her destination a secret from someone who knew her.

A few more twists and turns and Red found herself standing on the steps in front of Caganasti's magic shop. She recognized the sigil scrawled on the white sign, a leering face in black ink with swirls of color across the cheeks and a tuft on top that could be stylized hair. There were no words on the sign in any language that she could read. The shop could be selling anything, but as she stood outside, she felt a strong sense of wrongness creep over her. She shouldn't be here. She shouldn't be thinking about going inside. She should turn right around and go back home.

Red shook her head, the threads of magic hard to shake free. She had taken two steps back down the stairs, body obeying the command in the spell.

"Oh hells no," she grumbled, took the stairs two at time, and threw herself at the door before she could change her mind. She elbowed the door open, and only instincts honed by years of paying attention to every small noise allowed her to associate the sound of crossbolts being released in her general direction in the doorway. She fell to the floor, managed to catch the bag before the Book slid out, held it tightly in front of her body, and rolled to a crouch next to the door. She looked up to see two cross-bolts buried in the wooden door, a swirl of holes evidence that she wasn't the only one to receive such a welcome. As she watched, the bolts wavered and faded away, leaving new holes behind. She got slowly to her feet, ears tuned for more attacks. When nothing came shooting at her, she risked a cautious, "Hello?"

"Go away," a disinterested voice said from the depths of the shop. "You're not wanted here."

"I have a meeting with Caganasti," she said, taking in her surroundings but unwilling to move into the center aisle in front of the door, which still stood open. The shop was divided in half by an empty aisle in front of the doorway with aisles of shelves spreading out to the left and right. She took in the row of blue bottles on the top shelf near her, some of the liquid within bubbling ominously. The middle shelf was stocked with pottery jars of various sizes and colors. The bottom shelf held stacks of blank paper. Red thought for a moment that the paper had writing on it, but as she squinted to read it, she saw that the pages were blank.

She shook her clear, trying to clear her eyes. She didn't often deal with magic. It couldn't be trusted. Then again, it was useful. And she needed this trade.

"Yeah, yeah," the voice said. "Everyone wants a meeting with Caganasti. Go away."

Red was tired of playing this game. She pulled the Book from the bag and stepped boldly into the center aisle. "Fine, then. I suppose you don't want this, then?"

She turned as if to go, and the door slammed shut in her face, trapping her inside.

"My dear!" the voice said, and it was much closer now. "I seem to be mistaken, Captain. It seems we do have an appointment after all."

Red kept her grip on the Book as she turned, not truly thinking the mage would attack her and steal it, but wary enough to be cautious. The elf who stood before her was enough to make her pause for a moment, and she had seen all manner of peoples in her travels. He was tall for an elf, but his height was the least interesting thing about it. The elf had a shaved scalp except for a tall topknot of black hair that sprouted into long dredlocks that reached halfway down his back. His cheeks were swirled with tattoos, dark marks crawling across the pale skin down his face and neck and disappearing beneath the robes he wore. The tattoos were lovely, but Red had seen them before. She had even seen shaved heads and topknots, though not among the elves. What she hadn't seen were the small silver pins that ran through the skin of his forearms, glinting in the light from the lantern sitting on the counter. Red wondered what they were for, then decided that she didn't need to know. It was probably something magical that she would never quite understand.

She displayed the Book, careful to only touch the covers with her bare skin, knowing better than to touch the actual pages. "I believe you had some interest in this," she said.

Caganasti considered the Book, eyes seeing far more than she thought she ever would in the simple cover. He noticed how she held it. "I might," he offered blandly, "for the right price."

"You know my price," she told him, voice flat.

The elf nodded, then gestured at the Book. "May I?"

"You may look," she said and let him take it from her. She resisted the urge to wipe her hands on her pants, trying to keep the relief from showing on her face. It never paid to be too eager to trade. Then again, from what she heard of Caganasti, the elf was a straight dealer. They had already agreed to terms in the letters. She would be surprised if he tried to change the deal now.

The mage took the Book from her and walked to the back of the shop, laying it open on the counter and flipping through a few pages. After a long moment, he nodded, and then looked up. "It is the Book of Samander, as promised."

Red nodded, glad that the price Jocelyn had paid for the Book back in Warin had been worth it. "And the amulet?" she prompted.

Caganasti looked away for a moment, clearly contemplating. Red didn't like that look. "What?" she asked.

"There has been a slight difficulty with delivery," he said carefully.

"What does that mean?" Red asked, suddenly reminded of a green crewman trying to explain why his knot had come untied in rough seas. "Do you have the amulet?"

"I know where it is," Caganasti said helpfully.

"You mean it's not here," Red said, voice showing her displeasure. "This was not the deal we made."

"I know, and I regret the inconvenience." He paused for a moment, then seemed struck by an idea. "Are you married to the idea of an amulet?" he asked, and Red heard the salesman in his voice. He made his way to one of the shelves and retrieved a large wooden box. He placed it on the counter before her.

As Red watched, the image of a lovely redheaded girl swirled away, faded, and was replaced by a tall man with white blond hair and a smile that Red remembered. She stared at the magic box, not sure what was happening. Caganasti chuckled. "It is a Djinni Box. You see what you wish to see on the outside, and when you open it, you release that form into the world." He smirked at the man on the cover. "Djinni are fully physical beings, with all of the depth that you can give them. I imagine this man would give you great pleasure and delightful conversation."

Red stared at the box, then back at the elf. She could feel the heat creeping into her cheeks. "Why would I want some kind of sex box?" she asked.

"It's not merely a tool for sex," the elf said, "though I find it curious that your mind went there first. Djinni are complete people for as long as you wish them to be. The uses of such a Box are nearly endless."

"And what would I do with a djinni?" Red asked, still not understanding why he would show her this box.

"It's not about the djinni," he explained. "It's the fact that the djinni can appear as anyone that you wish." He gave her a long look. "Is that not what you want the amulet for? To change the appearance of someone?"

Red nodded. "Yes. To change *my* appearance."

"Oh!" Caganasti nodded as if this thought hadn't occurred to him. "I thought you simply wanted the appearance of a specific person. With the djinni, you could have that person's form at will... and without personal risk to yourself." He nodded again. "But you mean to appear as another, not to send in another with a different appearance. I see." He gathered the box from the counter and walked it back down the aisle, placing it carefully on the shelf again.

He came back to her slowly, face furrowed in thought. He glanced at the Book again, and Red heard the sound of what might be another door in the back of the shop open and close. There was no sound of crossbolts, so Red assumed the newcomer must be expected. Caganasti nodded once at the sound, looked at her, then back at the Book. He nodded more firmly. "I may have a solution."

"Go on," Red told him.

"The amulet you seek is not far from here."

"In the city?" she prompted.

"Not quite." He gave her a long look. "Are you familiar with Noam?"

Red thought for a moment. The name was familiar. "You mean the Noam who lives in the mountains north of the city?"

Caganasti nodded. "She has the amulet. I sent someone to bring it down the mountain to me, but I don't think he made it there. Noam sent a message that no one had arrived yet, and that was three days ago." He shook his head. "So hard to find good couriers these days. And the mountains are treacherous."

"You mean for me to travel to Noam and retrieve the amulet myself?" she asked, voice tinged with annoyance. This had not been the agreement.

"How delightful of you to volunteer!" Caganasti exclaimed. He slid the Book across the counter to himself, and suddenly it was covered up completely, a wrapped package that no longer emanated the magic that had been making Red's skin tingle. He handed the package back to her and helped her slide it back into the pack. "Bring her this as well. Consider it payment for the trade."

Red started to balk, to argue that she had not agreed on a trek through the mountains, amulet be damned, but Caganasti was still talking. "Excellent. You will need winter gear, of course. The season has turned. And you will not go alone."

Red cut him off, his patronizing tone getting the better of her sensibilities. "I will of course go alone!" she snapped. "Who would go with me? You?"

"No, not me," Caganasti said, face lit with something like hilarity at the idea. "I am not suited for hikes through dangerous terrain." He made a broad gesture to the man who stepped out from the back room of the shop. "But he certainly is."

"My lady," said Lord Stefan Grayson, bowing deeply, "I am pleased to be of service."

<hr/>

"You're sure it's just over the ridge?" Red asked, cheeks tingling in the biting wind as she squinted across the snow. She tried again to find the sun, to orient herself, but the damn snow was making everything so bright it was impossible to see. She needed nightfall so she could find her way by the stars. Red knew the map of the night stars better than she knew her own reflection. This far north, she should see Old Mother low on the horizon with Tyrion's Garter just above and to the right.

That is, if we are even going in the right direction.

Stefan had pulled out the compass again, holding it aloft as if that made it more effective amid the mountains, and checked their heading. He relied on that contraption way more than Red liked. Yes, some of them were marvelous creations, able to track the directions without flaw, but Red had seen far too many that were seriously incompetent, only able to spin prettily in their fine casing but without any connection to the world outside. Red only trusted the stars to tell her the truth. A craftsman who had never left the safety and comfort of his shop was just as likely to make an inaccurate timepiece and call it a compass. He would never need to truly rely on it. Red would trust the sun far more than the compass, but the glare from the ice-covered snow made it impossible to judge the direction, enmeshed in the mountains as they were. "It is that way," he said, and the confidence in his voice irked her, as everything he did or said since they left Firene two days ago irked her.

This whole trip irked her. She had grown so accustomed to being short with him that she didn't recall what it was to be pleasant. If Lady Black were there, her friend would have called her out on her behavior, no doubt suggesting that her own poor attitude had more to do with lack of satisfaction than lack of direction. Lady Black thought every bad day could be solved with a good time between the sheets.

Red stole a sideways glance at Lord Stefan. His face was nearly bloodless, the cold air pulling the heat from him as they walked, the strands of white hair around his face giving him an ethereal air despite the brown hat pulled down to cover his ears. He looked nearly Elven, Red decided, taking after the people he had spent so much time around the last few months.

Though she had been curt with him, they had still talked on the way up the mountain. He had told her how the taxes on Ruyian wine had brought him to Firene to settle negotiations, but how the people had liked him well enough to keep him on for the next round of discussions. He was still representing his House, but it was more than that now. Lord Stefan Grayson was moving up in the world in his own right, pedigree or not. He enjoyed the work, but there were times when it was challenging. Stefan had been secretive about his reason for accompanying her to see Noam. There was no way it was pure chivalry. Red knew a deal when she saw one, and Caganasti and Stefan had shaken on something as they left the shop. She thought it must be something magical, perhaps an aid to help him in his negotiations.

He had pressed her about the package she carried, but since it no longer resembled the Book she had carried into the shop, Red was able to keep him guessing.

"Is it not enough to simply allow that we both have our reasons to see Noam? We are hardly paramours sharing secrets."

Stefan had given her a look after that, some slight color entering his pale skin despite the cold. "Are we not familiars, then?" he had whispered in a voice that sent a shiver through her skin.

"Are we?" she asked him, looking around at the snow-capped mountains around them. "Is this your idea of a tryst then?"

The days had passed in a blur of snark and sparks as they moved carefully around one another. He knew she had her own ship these days, but not what port she called home or what business kept her ship afloat. She could tell that the idea of her independence attracted him.

A wave of longing for her ship made her pause again, shielding her eyes from the ever-present glare and looking behind them, down the long mountainside. She could see the white blur of snow and the black stone peeking through, but she wasn't quite sure if the white blur far away was the city of Firene. She tried to imagine that it was, and that blue on the edge was her ship still neatly docked. No doubt Lady Black had had to pay triple their expected fees for the extra days in the city. She really hoped the amulet was worth this trouble.

"It is this way," Stefan said, calling her back to the present, and she turned away from the city below.

"Is it? You've been here before, have you? Recognize that cliffside?" Red hated the bitterness in her voice, but she was made for the rocking deck of a ship at sea, not the frozen carcass of a mountain.

"Not particularly," Stefan remarked, "but Caganasti gave very specific directions." He took off over a small rise, and she watched his body disappear over the other side. He didn't seem to be sliding off to his death, so that was a good sign. She waited for the rope around her waist to pull taut before following him. She understood such precautions—she had done similar things during storms at sea—but it still bothered her to be tied to him so literally. The rope had come in handy though as they climbed up the steeper parts of the path. Red had thanked her skills at climbing ropes slick with seawater more than once as they made their way here.

She cleared the rise, and then she could see it: a small tuft of smoke coming from within a cluster of fir trees to the left. A few more steps revealed the small wooden structure tucked amid the trees. Red thought it might be a nice place to have a home when the weather was pleasant. Now, it just looked like a place to huddle away from the winter air.

Stefan gave her a look as if to say, "See?" but he didn't say anything as they approached the cottage. The walls were wood, but the roof looked to be made of tin. Red wondered how Noam managed to avoid freezing to death in this remote place. Sure, there was a fire, but the place looked flimsy. In fact, if there hadn't been smoke, she might have mistaken the place for an abandoned hunter's shack.

"What a lovely home," Red remarked sarcastically.

Stefan gave her a look, but before he could speak, a voice rang out, "You may find it more appealing to your tastes after you've come inside."

The door of the small building opened to reveal an old woman bundled in layers of woven scarves and animal hide cloak. Her hair was pure white, pushed back from her face by a red band, and though her skin was lined with wrinkles and her body hunched with age, her eyes were bright and calculating, the eyes of an old woman who saw far more than she would ever let on.

Red approached, walking up to the doorway behind Stefan. He bowed formally to the woman who must be Noam, "Your servant, ma'am," and Red had to restrain the urge to follow suit with a curtsy. She forced her body to stay upright and held out her hand to the woman in greeting, the introduction of an equal. The woman's skin was warm, her hand strong.

"Welcome," she said in the voice of a far younger woman. "Do come in."

"Are you in the habit of offering hospitality to vagrants?" Red asked, following Noam inside.

"You're hardly strangers, Lady Serena and Lord Stefan." Red jerked a little at her true name spoken aloud for the second time in the last three days. "And Caganasti sent word of your coming."

"So you know why we are here then?" Red asked, happy to dispense with the pleasantries and get down to business. She thought there may be a few hours of daylight left, not enough to get far down the mountain but enough to get started.

"Oh yes," Noam said, shutting the door against the cold as Stefan followed them inside.

"Great!" Red started to continue but stopped dead as she looked at the room they now occupied. From the outside, the shack might have a single room large enough for a bed, a small table, a firepit, and a tiny circle of open floor. But they stood in a lavish parlor that would rival the best House in Firene. The chairs looked comfortable, and the material was fine. There was a fire crackling merrily in a fireplace, and there were two doors through which Red could see a well-appointed dining room and kitchen. To the right, a set of stairs climbed to another floor. She knew what the place looked like from the outside. There was no way there was a second floor. She looked at Stefan, who was calculating the differences as well, and then to Noam.

"You have a lovely home," she told Noam without a trace of sarcasm.

"I thank you for the compliment," the old woman said, then gestured for them to take off their cloaks. Once they had disrobed enough to sit down, Noam disappeared with their winter gear and returned with a tray holding a teapot and three mugs. She set this down on the small table in the center of the chairs and gestured for them to take a seat. Red claimed an overstuffed armchair near the fire, and Stefan took the one across from her, also near the fire. His cheeks were flushed, life and feeling coming back in, and Red tried to surreptitiously stretch out her toes towards the flames. Her boots were of the best quality, waterproof for the worst ocean weather, but they were not lined for the cold, and her toes were frozen.

Noam held out a mug to her, and Red accepted, resisting the urge to wonder where this tea had come from. This wasn't a meeting where she had to worry about poison. Caganasti may have altered their arrangement, but the elf was trustworthy. He would not send her up here to be killed. She took a small sip just as Stefan did, and she could see that he had the same brief debate with himself before tasting. Poison wasn't common among the elves—they usually survived such assassination attempts—but he had come from Ruyan, where political intrigue was an art form, and it was hard to forget such habits. The tea was delicious, warming her belly without burning her lips, and she sank into the chair, allowing the physical comfort to lull her for a long moment.

Noam let them sit in silence for a time, enjoying the heat and refreshment, then she invited them into the dining room where the table was laden with enough fare to delight a true foodie and set for three. They passed the evening with small talk of this and that, but no words of the business that brought them there. Red was pleasantly surprised to find that the lager was stout and the food was flavorful. She was accustomed to the much simpler fare available on board her ship.

Stefan asked about the messenger who had failed to return to Firene.

"He didn't just fail to return," Noam said, dipping a hunk of bread into her soup and taking a bite. "Poor lad didn't even show up at all." She shook her head. "I don't mean to disparage him, poor soul. The mountain is treacherous."

"Rest his soul?" Stefan asked. "You believe him dead then?"

Noam nodded, taking another bite. "I know him to be dead." She sighed. "There's a bear roaming about, a bogan, far too late in the season for such aggressive behavior, but this one's tricky. I imagine I'll have to find it soon and put it down."

Red shuddered at the idea of such a huge creature wandering freely in the place where she had so recently traveled. Creatures of the sea did not cause her fear, but she had heard stories of the brown bears who lived in the mountains, creatures twice as tall as she and weighing half a ton. She had seen their claws, each one as long as her entire hand, for sale in enough marketplaces, noted the old bloodstains that coated each one with awe. "We didn't see any bears," she commented, then looked at Stefan. "Did you see bear sign?"

He shrugged and nodded. "During my watch last night, I heard something shuffling nearby. I scared it with the fire, and it moved on."

Red felt her face redden with fear and outrage. "Why didn't you wake me?"

"Because I could handle it," he replied. "I mean no offense, my lady. I know that you would be an asset in any confrontation. I didn't think it needful to alarm you." He took a final spoonful of his soup and then dabbed his mouth with the napkin. He felt her still looking at him, so he added, "And I recall how you feel about bears."

"You... recall..." Red started, then realized what he meant. They had had very few conversations in her father's parlor, but one topic they had discussed was the bear rug on the floor. Red had made it clear that she thought the only good bear was a dead bear. "I see," she said.

"'The only way to treat a bear is to skin it,'" Stefan quoted, and Red blushed.

Noam had been looking back and forth between them, an amused smirk on her face. "I don't completely agree with that sentiment, having no issue with most of the bear population on this mountain, but this bear in particular needs to be put down. If the skin can be useful, then so be it."

"Would you like me to hunt it for you?" Stefan offered. "When the sun rises—"

"No, child, no need," Noam interrupted, and Red smirked at the thought of anyone calling Stefan a child. He was nearing five and fifty. "He will be gone soon enough." She looked at both of them, seeing that they were finished eating, and at a gesture, the food on the table faded.

"That's a neat trick," Red observed. "The galley wenches would love it."

Noam nodded but then shook her head. "Not likely. It's just pretty magic. It moves the dishes to the kitchen. Your wenches would still have to wash them."

"Would you like some help?" Red asked, not thrilled at the notion but prompted by her notion of reciprocity.

Noam laughed, a genuine belly laugh. "You think I don't have the magic to wash them as well? I may move them with parlor tricks, but I'm too old to be scrubbing in the kitchen." She laughed again. "No, Captain, you need not get your hands wet." Noam stood up from the table. "Now to business." She gestured to the door. "I find it best to speak in the parlor."

They settled into the chairs around the low table in front of the fire. Noam spoke first to Red. "I believe you have something for me."

Red reached for her bag and withdrew the wrapped bundle. She placed it on the table. Noam reached out to touch it, and it started to glow. The shape rearranged itself, and the Book appeared. Red felt the tingle of magic on her skin and leaned back. She heard Stefan take a quick breath, looked up, and saw the avid way his eyes looked at the Book. He looked at Red, then back down at the book again, as if unable to believe that this was the thing she had been carrying.

"The Book of Samander," Noam breathed. The old woman looked from Red to Stefan, an unreadable expression on her face. "Long has it been sought after."

"Yes," Stefan whispered, and Red gave him an odd look. As far as she knew, Stefan didn't have magic. *Why is he so fixated on a Book that clearly reeks of the stuff?*

"But fair trade first," Noam snapped, and Stefan looked up from the Book, face focused on the conversation again. But there was an eagerness in his eyes that did not fade. "The amulet." She stood up and walked to a small cabinet against the wall. She opened the top drawer and withdrew a small pendant on a silver chain. She displayed it to Red, draping the chain so that the small silver figure at the end fell across the back of her hand.

"The Amulet of Naseri." She tugged the chain so the amulet slid from side to side on her hand. Red thought that the small stylized figure of a woman shifted slightly as it moved, but it must be the firelight. She reached out to take it from Noam. The old woman let her have it but not without a stern warning. "You know what it does, yes?"

Red nodded. "It alters the appearance of the wearer."

"But do you know in what manner?"

"I don't imagine that it comes with a user manual," Red quipped, "but I thought I could figure it out."

"No need," Noam told her. "It has two primary uses. The first one is the one you seek—it will make you appear as you wish." She gestured for Red to put the amulet on.

Red could feel the slight tingle of magic as it settled around her neck. She looked at Noam and Stefan. "What do I look like?"

"Like you," Stefan said, and Noam chuckled.

"You must concentrate on the person you wish to impersonate." Red thought for a moment of Lady Black, of her dark skin and wild braids. Stefan sucked in his breath, and Red looked down, surprised to see that her normally pale hands were now dark. She shook her head, watching the braids move against her chest, but not feeling the weight of them as she expected to. She touched her hair. "I still feel like me," she said, "but I look like her."

Noam nodded. "'Twill take some practice to get it right," she said. "You should practice in front of a mirror. If you are wearing smaller clothing, but the image is wearing a formal gown, you will have to learn to move as though you are wearing the gown. You will need to think about your hands, lest they disappear into the glamour."

Red nodded, letting the thoughts of Lady Black fade away, seeing her own hands in her lap again. "Thank you," she said, and Noam was turning to Stefan, when she said, "Wait!"

Noam turned back to her. "Yes?"

"You said it had two uses. What is the other?"

"Are you familiar with the tale of Naseri?"

Red laughed a little. "What, like the goddess of lust?"

Noam nodded. "The very same."

"What about her?"

"What do you know of her?" Noam countered.

Red considered. She read the tales as a young girl, heard more lascivious versions as an adult, but they all boiled down the same story. "Naseri appears as the heart's desire of the beloved," she said. "She has no form of her own; she is whatever you want her to be—man or woman or anything in between. She lives on the desire of others, never settling down with one person, always seeking the one who can set free her true form."

"And that is her Amulet," Noam said, pointing to the necklace Red now wore.

"So, what? I can be someone's heart's desire?" She couldn't keep the skepticism from her voice. Most people Red had met had no idea what they truly desired; she didn't think an amulet would know.

"Exactly," Noam said with enough certainty to make Red believe her.

Red thought about what people said they wanted and how this feature could be useful... but also dangerous. It did not always end well for those who gave another their most secret wish. She looked at Noam, wanting to try it out all the same. *What do you desire?* She focused, and suddenly her body shifted. She could feel that she was different, but she couldn't tell how. "What do you see?" she asked them.

"I'll never tell," Noam whispered, enough playfulness in her voice to remind Red that she hadn't always been an old woman living alone.

Red looked over at Stefan who was now staring at her in the way he had been staring at the Book earlier. "What do you see, my lord?" *What do you desire?*

His lip quivered, but his voice was strong. "I see you, my lady."

"Hmm." Red shook herself, that different feeling fading away. "I must need practice."

Noam chuckled softly. "Be careful, my dear," the old woman cautioned. "It does not do to be other people too often, lest one forget oneself in the process."

Red nodded in agreement, tucking the amulet underneath her shirt. "I will," she promised, thinking of Naseri's true form, and how none of her lovers ever saw her as she truly was. She remembered the djinni in the box back at Caganasti's shop and wondered how such a creature came to be trapped in a box, then she stopped herself. It would not do to dwell on such matters. She had the amulet in her possession, and now she could expand her business. It was enough.

"And now, my lord, your trade?" Noam asked, turning to Stefan.

From within his bag, he withdrew a smaller pouch, unlaced the top, and pulled out a small glass bottle. The liquid inside seemed thick and glowed a strange mixture of blue and purple, colors chasing themselves across the glass in the firelight. He set the bottle on the table and slid it over to Noam with one delicate finger. "Well, well," Noam muttered. "Tonight is just full of old delights." She gave Stefan a discerning look. "This must have cost a pretty penny."

"I have been assured that it is worth every cent," he suggested, and Red saw the negotiator in him ready to begin the dance.

"Indeed it is," she agreed, picking up the bottle and moving it gently side to side, letting the liquid swirl into a kaleidoscope of colors that made Red slightly dizzy. The colors faded slightly, replaced by something like foam, a sudsy liquid that slid up the sides of the bottle. "You are sure that you want this trade?"

Stefan nodded, seeming undisturbed by the light show.

Noam looked down at the Book, still sitting on the table. "It is dangerous for one like you."

"Life is dangerous," Stefan commented. "I will be careful."

"You will be dead," Noam snapped, all traces of the benevolent old woman faded, replaced by one long used to suffering fools, "though I realize that will not change your mind." She sighed, then pushed the Book over to him.

Stefan reached for it, then coughed politely. "Could you...?"

Noam smiled, reached out, touched the Book, and Red watched as it folded into itself, reforming into the smaller bundle she had carried up the mountain. She was glad to feel the magic fade away. The tingle of the amulet against her skin was pleasant; the Book had made her teeth ache. Stefan tucked it away into his bag.

Noam stood and nodded to each of them in turn. "Now I bid you goodnight," she said. Red glanced around the room, and Noam must have read her face for she nodded to the right, and Red saw a door that she hadn't noticed before. "Make yourselves comfortable in the guest room." Through the new door, Red could see the drapery surrounding a double bed.

She glanced at Stefan, then back at Red. "I'm fine right here," she insisted, pushing away images of a shirtless Stefan lying next to her. "Do you have a blanket?"

Noam nodded at the pile of pillow and blanket that suddenly appeared on the chair next to Red. "Thanks," she told the old woman as she tugged the wool quilt over herself and slid down in the chair.

"Good evening, madam," Stefan said to Noam, inclining his head in respect. Noam left, walking up the stairs and disappearing from view. He looked at Red, wrapped up and settled in her chair. "You cannot be serious," he commented. "Take the bed."

"It's fine," Red said. "You are accustomed to comfort. I wouldn't take that from you."

Stefan rolled his eyes at her, then turned away and walked into the guest room. Red thought he was going to shut the door and be done with her, but he emerged a moment later with the blanket from the bed and another pillow. He settled himself into the chair across from her in pointed silence.

"Don't be foolish," Red finally said. "One of us should be comfortable. This whole place is magic. I bet that bed is amazing."

"Beds alone aren't amazing," Stefan said, and then added uncharacteristically, "Companions make them so."

"I imagine you must have had many amazing bedfellows then," Red retorted. "I am happy for you."

"Are you then? I imagine you have had your share of companions, alone on that ship in the middle of the ocean."

"There is something to be said for the rocking of a ship at sea," she admitted. Stefan's normally pale face grew even paler. He looked away from her to the fireplace as if trying to forget something unpleasant. "Oh come on," she coaxed, leaning forward and letting the blanket fall to her waist. "You mean to say you've never had some fun in a berth aboard ship? I imagine such things are usually reserved for the bedrooms of noble Houses, but ships have a way of making everything seem more romantic."

"If that were true," Stefan said, "you would be married by now."

"I spoke of romance, my lord," Red commented drily, "not marriage."

"And those are not the same thing in your experience?"

Red laughed, the sound spilling up from her belly in a raucous bellow. "You mean to tell me that you find marriage to be conducive to amazing bedfellows? Most men I've known find way more satisfaction outside of the marital bed than in it."

"I would not know," Stefan snapped, "having never been married."

"Well you've certainly been on a ship and know what I'm talking about, then."

Stefan shook his head. "I have been on a ship, my lady, but there is nothing romantic about it."

Red sat up, leaning in toward him, face reddening. "How dare you insult my ship?"

"I said nothing of your ship, my lady," he said, sitting up and leaning toward her.

"But the ocean," she whispered, "the wind in your hair and nothing on the horizon but the water…" She let the words trail off, missing her ship with everything in her, missing the nights she had spent on deck with this or that lover staring at the engorged moon reflecting on the dark water. "It is … spectacular."

Stefan had reached out to touch her hand, and he used that to pull her to him, closing the distance between them. She leaned forward even more and the amulet came out from beneath her collar, the silver glinting in the firelight. Red had the sudden urge to know what Stefan truly wanted, to see what he desired. There was a low thrum of magic, but then it faded. She waited for his reaction, but his face hadn't changed. He was staring at her, transfixed.

"What do you see, my lord?" she asked, voice husky with desire.

"I see you, my lady," he said, and then he kissed her.

***

"I thank you again for everything," Stefan told Noam. "You have been a most gracious host."

The old woman nodded. "I am happy to oblige when you bring me such delightful things."

Red thought about asking about the bottle but decided she had a better chance of getting the information from Stefan than Noam. She glanced at him, clothes impeccable in the morning light, that silky smooth hair perfectly brushed around his face, that lovely face.

Noam opened the door, then turned back and caught the expression on Red's face as she watched Stefan gather his things. "Ah," the old woman mused, "young love."

"Do we look young to you?" Red asked in a low voice. "And this is not love."

"Is it not?" Noam considered. "I see respect and friendship and trust. I have seen marriages built on far less."

"Nothing kills love faster than marriage," Red commented, and Noam chuckled.

"Ah yes, ever the cynic," she observed, then nodded at Stefan when he reached them at the door.

"Serena a cynic?" he repeated, catching the end of the conversation. "I would never believe such a thing!"

They left the shelter of Noam's cottage, heading down the mountain with the morning sun at their backs. The journey was pleasant, the two of them stealing moments to touch whenever possible—a hand hold here as they crossed a narrow ledge, a solid grip on her hips as he helped across a small gap—enjoying the novelty of being able to touch one another.

Red tried to avoid thinking about what would happen when they got back to the city, tried to forget the impending separation. She thought of the one night they would have as they made their way down the mountain and tried to pay attention to their surroundings until the sky began to darken.

They were nearing the halfway point, and Red's attention had wandered from the snow-slick ground to the fire they would soon build and to the promise of the cool night air warmed by Stefan's touch, when she heard the sounds. There was the loud snap of a wet branch, a heavy step trodding too heavily in the snow behind them, and then Stefan was shouting and she was pushed aside as something huge rushed between them. Red caught herself quickly, her reflexes accustomed to quickly shifting ground, and she skidded to a halt and spun to face the threat. Stefan had done the same on the other side of the clearing, hands moving with a grace that she hadn't imagined as he drew his short sword and adopted a solid battle stance. She knew Stefan had trained with weapons, but she had never seen him fight. He seemed prepared enough.

She drew her own club from the straps of the bag on her back and held it comfortably in both hands, ready to take down the foe with blunt force.

The brown bear turned around, the energy from its charge diverted, and bellowed at the two of them. Red felt her skin prickle with excitement and disgust. A bear. A bear was bellowing in front of her, about to charge, and she was going to bludgeon it to death with her club and walk on its hide every day for the rest of her life. She set her heels into the snow and waited for the charge.

The bear looked from her to Stefan and back again, then charged at Stefan, deciding he was the bigger target. She swung at it as it went by, her club making a satisfying sound as she scored a hit on its back, but clearly doing little damage to the huge creature. Stefan dodged to his right, sword striking the beast as it passed, but not enough to take it down, not enough to block the claw that raked down his shoulder and arm. He cried out but held onto his sword, managing to shift it to his other hand as the bear turned for another swipe. Red cursed at the sight of the blood pouring down Stefan's sleeve, spattering the white snow, and charged at the bear's back, hitting the bear with all of her strength. She pivoted back from another blow with the club and kicked the bear under its hind legs. It screamed in rage and turned to face her.

Red was a solid fighter, having earned her stripes in countless bar brawls, but she had never faced a raging bear. She did the only thing she could think of: she swung her club at its face with everything in her, swinging from the hips as she had been taught, focusing on the bear's jaw. She felt the impact up her arm and knew that her shoulder would ache for a week, but it was the sound that she would never forget, the wet snapping crunch of bone as she smashed the bear's head. The creature took another two steps toward her, but it was only momentum, the crushed skull a sure sign that she had won. The carcass fell heavily to the snow-covered ground, and she took a few steps around it to check on Stefan. He had fallen to one knee, sword discarded on the ground and one hand pressed to the wounds in his shoulder and arm.

Red knelt next to him, pushing his hand aside to assess the damage. She bade him sit, then used her knife to cut away the remains of his shirt. She gave the wound a critical eye, pressing gently and efficiently here and there, and nodded, giving Stefan exact instructions on where to press as she rifled through her bag for what she would need. Accidents were common onboard. Red never went anywhere without her medical kit.

She would need a fire to prepare her tools and to keep him warm as she worked. Her hands shook a little as she withdrew her flint and steel from her bag, and she took a precious moment to calm her mind. A long breath later, she struck the first spark into a small pile of damp branches, trusting her starter cotton to catch the bigger wood.

Her hands were steady as she prepared her needle. Stefan gritted his teeth when she sewed the longest gash down his arm, but he didn't cry out. She gave him some water to drink, watching as he took a few sips with his good arm, hand shaking a little bit but not terribly. She had seen such cuts before, but those were the effect of broken beams on ship; she thought that bear claws may heal differently, but she had done what she could. Now she could only keep him comfortable until the morning and then help him down the mountain.

He lay down for a time, letting her set up their makeshift camp around the fire she had hastily built. She dragged the bear carcass as far away as she could, knowing it would attract other predators but hoping there weren't any nearby. The bear had killed most of the wildlife in the area. She thought they would be safe for one night.

After she laid out her bedroll and sat down near the fire, Red checked Stefan's arm. She had wrapped him in her spare cloak, not willing to ruin one of his beautiful shirts with blood. She could buy ten new cloaks for what Stefan's clothes cost. When they got back down to the city, he could buy her a new one. The wound seemed clean, his skin moist and comfortably warm, but Red knew how fast the swelling and fever could creep in. She felt his face, and his eyes fluttered open. She was glad to see only Stefan's eyes, untinged by the glaze of sickness but made heavy with pain.

He looked around the clearing, spotted the trail where she had dragged the bear's body away, and looked back at her. "That was quite a swing," he observed, and she was glad to hear that his voice was strong.

"You weren't so bad yourself," she told him.

He looked down at his arm. "Not good enough."

"You're alive and the bear is not. Good enough," she disagreed.

Stefan nodded his agreement, but then he reached out to touch her face with his good arm. He looked at the sky, where the sun had started to set below the mountain, and sighed heavily, wincing as the movement jarred his shoulder. "This is not how I imagined this night," he commented.

Red grinned ruefully. "Nor I, but I'd rather have you alive with a dead bear than be distracted out here and then have a bear show up." She shook her head. "I'm amazed that we made it up the mountain without getting attacked. That creature was wild."

Stefan moved as if to shrug but stopped himself halfway. "It hunted us on the way up but never got too close. I do not think it would have approached the fire."

"Maybe," she allowed, "but I'm glad we were together to face it. I've been in some fights in my time, but nothing like that."

"You were magnificent," he told her, face lighting up when she smiled at him.

"I was terrified," she admitted, "but it's done now. I don't usually fight monsters; I fight people." She looked around at the emptiness surrounding them. "And here we are, alone on the mountainside."

"There is no one else I would rather be with," Stefan said, and she felt her face warm.

"Nor I," she said, and though she wanted to say more, she didn't. *What can I say?*

"Stay with me," Stefan said.

Red looked around their camp. "Where would I go?"

"No. I mean stay. With me."

Red sat back, heart heavy in her chest. "You know I cannot."

He sighed, looking away from her into the fire.

"But you could come with me," she suggested, trying not to imagine Lady Black's face if she came aboard with Lord Stefan. "You did say you've never found ships romantic. I could change your mind."

Stefan chuckled, then winced at the movement. "Tempting, but no. I cannot."

"I could wait until your business with the elves is concluded. I could bring you back to Upsen or even Rasa. It's a lovely journey."

"I believe you," he said, face tight with something else.

"But you cannot," she repeated, reading his reluctance and feeling her heart sink even further. "I understand."

He caught her hand with his good arm. "No, you do not." He looked away, grimaced, then faced her full on. "I get seasick," he admitted.

"What?" she asked.

"Seasick," he said again. "I cannot be on a boat. I spend the entire time heaving. It is not romantic in any way."

"Surely you could get over it," she encouraged. "I imagine the time you were sick, there may have been rough seas. It's not always like that."

He shook his head. "No, it is always like that. I have been on enough miserable voyages to know my limits." He grabbed her hand, fingers pressing into hers, willing her to understand. "It is why I have stayed in Firene. The fastest way to Upsen is via ship. I must wait until the season passes, and then I must travel overland to get there."

"But it's so dangerous," Red said. "The roads are filled with high-waymen. There are miles of wilderness." She glanced at the carcass across the clearing. "No doubt the path is filled with wild animals."

Stefan gave the same half shrug. "I will take my chances. Sea voyages and I do not mesh."

Red nodded. She knew they had no real future together, knew this was a brief fling, but she was an optimist at heart, and so she had hoped, just a little. That hope was gone. He could no more join her on her ship than she could leave the ocean and be his lady.

"You and I do not mesh," she said slowly, sadness tinging her words.

He gave her a rueful look. "We mesh just fine, my lady." He gave her a wicked grin, and she smiled in return. "I had hoped to mesh some more this evening, but I imagine that will not be."

Red shook her head. "You will need to be gentle on that arm," she told him. "Though I am glad we still have the night together. I do actually enjoy your company," she admitted, then added, "surprisingly enough."

He laughed. "Shall we watch the moon rise together then? It is no ship's deck, but we can look at the stars together."

Red smiled again. "Of course," she agreed, settling herself against his good side and staring up at the darkening sky. "We can talk about why you shouldn't trust that compass you have."

The next evening, Red and Stefan stood in the lane marking the division from city proper and the lower ward, staring at one another. Stefan was battered, eyes tired from the long trek down the mountain, but not ill as she had feared. He was strong. He would heal fine, especially now that he was back in the city.

"My lord," she said and curtseyed, "it has been my pleasure."

He bowed. "The pleasure has been all mine, Captain Red."

Red smiled at his use of her name. He had called her Serena while they travelled on the mountain, but that time was done, and she was Captain Red again.

"Perhaps we shall meet again, my lord, should you need a guide into the wilderness," she said.

"There is no greater traveling companion," he agreed. He gave her a look then. "Be careful, my lady. I want to recognize you if we meet again."

Red acknowledged the reference to her new amulet. "I will." She thought of the Book of Samander and repressed a shiver. "But you're the one who should be careful. That is no trifle you carry. Such things are gained at great peril."

"And here I thought you only wanted me for my charming good books," Stefan joked, but when she didn't laugh, he admitted, "It is not for me." He added, "It is something I intend to bargain with."

Red couldn't deny the relief she felt at this news. "I am glad to hear that," she told him, "but think carefully. That is dangerous in the wrong hands."

He nodded his agreement, accepting her warning as she had accepted his. She had to trust that he would make the right choice, just as he had to trust that she would.

When it seemed there was no more to say, he took a step toward her, and then she took a step toward him, and then they were kissing in the middle of the street. They parted after a long moment, and both were smiling.

"Fare thee well, my lady," Lord Stefan bid her.

"And you, my lord. Long days and pleasant nights."

"More pleasant when you are in port," he commented, and her smile grew. She nodded and started walking toward her ship. She still had some work to do before they left the city.

Three days later, Captain Red stood on the deck of the *Volant*, watching the sky as they prepared to leave port. They would have good weather, at least.

Lady Black stood at her side, long braids bound into a single tail down her back. "Ready to sail, Captain?"

Captain Red nodded, giving the signal to set off. It felt good to be back on her ship. She waited until they were well clear of the shore before heading down to her cabin. A large box sat on her bed. She called Lady Black.

"What is this?" she asked, gesturing to the package.

"A delivery for you," said her first mate. "It arrived this morning."

"Why didn't you tell me?"

"The courier said to keep it secret until we were away from shore."

Red gave her a look but sat down on the bed and opened the box. Inside was a perfectly preserved bearskin, just the right size for the floor of her cabin. The skull of the creature had been crushed. There was a note sitting on top of the rug, and she pulled it out, smiling.

To good times in the mountains, the note read. *Yours always.*

"I don't get it," Lady Black said, picking up the bear rug and examining it. "It's nice work, though. Who sent it? Don't they know you hate bears?"

"It's a long story," Red told her friend, spreading the bear rug on the floor and sitting down to admire it. "Did I ever tell you about my father's house?"

V

FAMILY TREES

HOUSE VAN KREEOSK

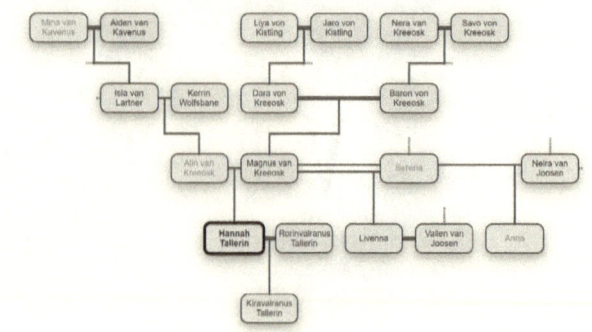

Focus: Hannah Tallerin

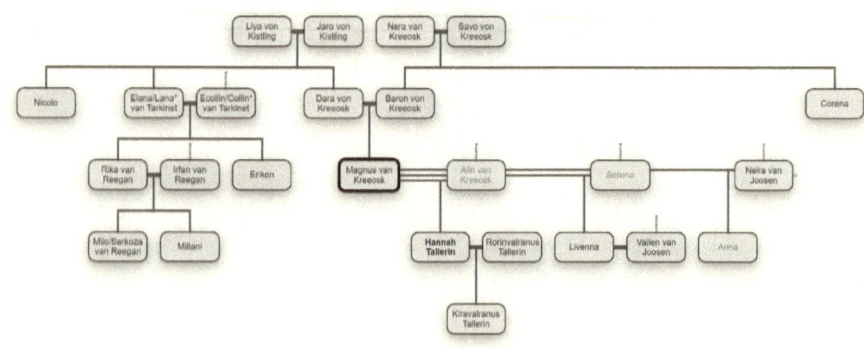

Focus: Magnus van Kreeosk

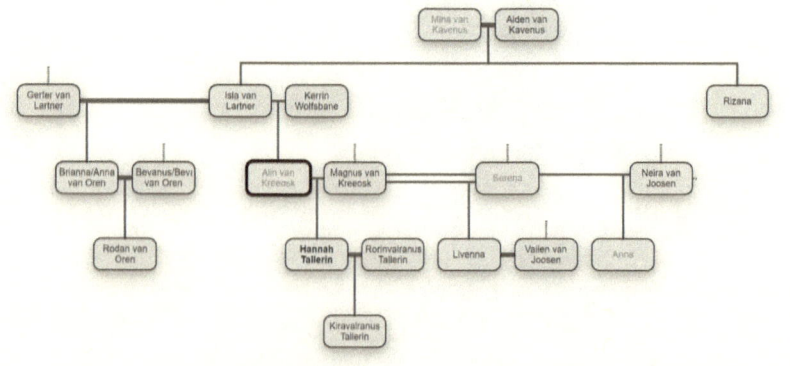

Focus: Alin van Kreeosk

HOUSE VAN KREEOSK, VAN REEGAN, AND VAN SHERINAK

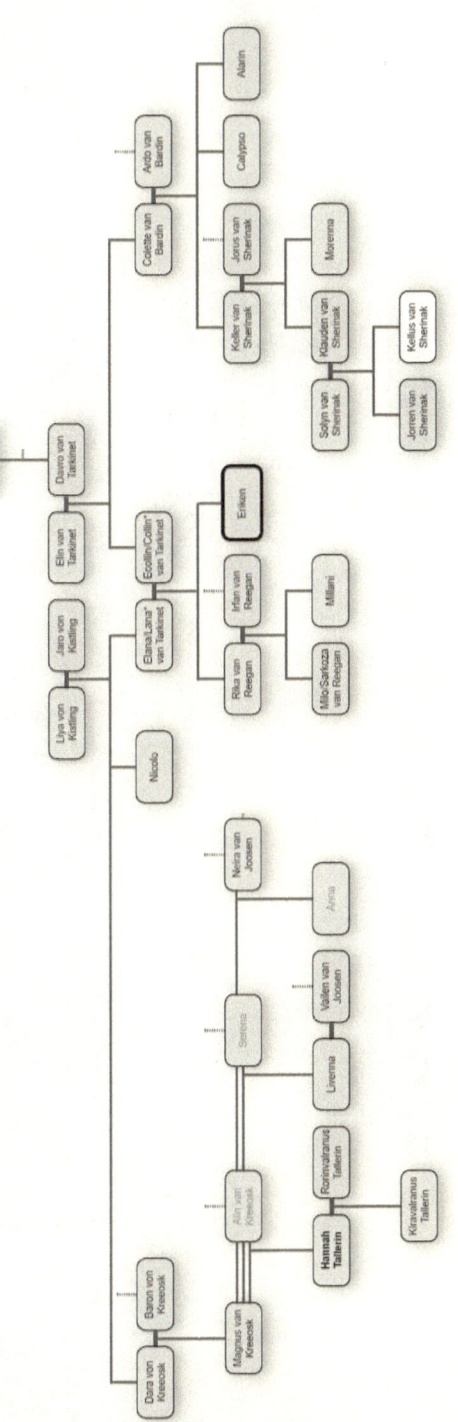

HOUSE VAN LARTNER

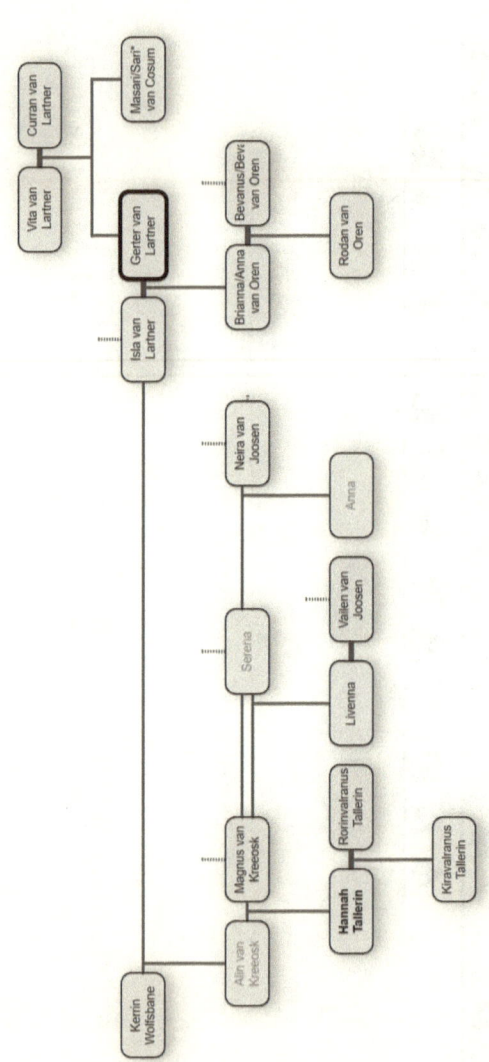

ANNA

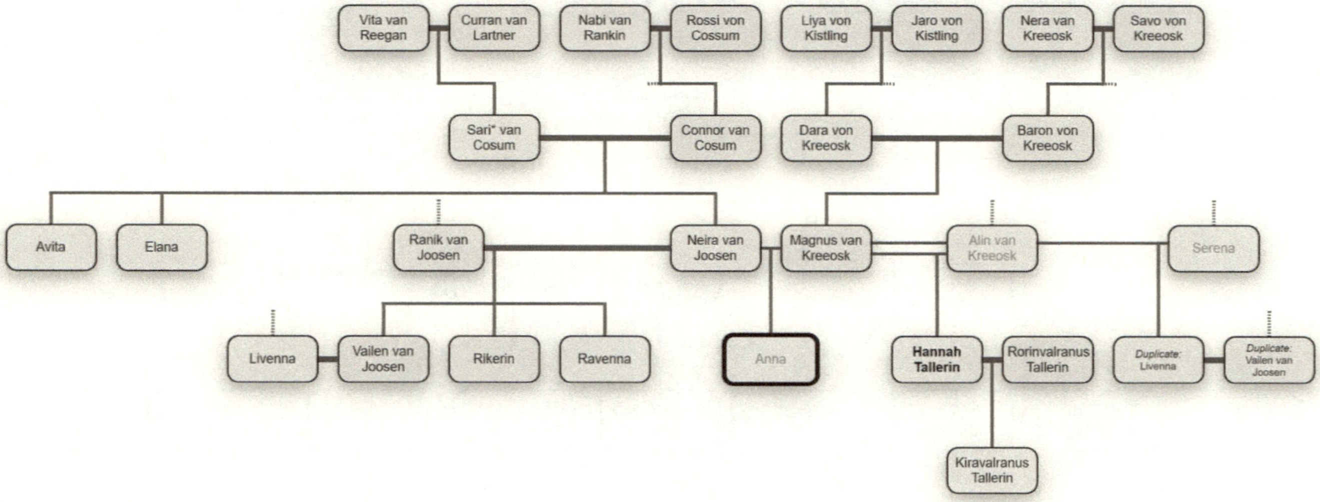

Savo von Kreeosk

Nera van Kreeosk

Baron von Kreeosk

Serena

Jaro von Kistling

Liya von Kistling

Dara von Kreeosk

Alin van Kreeosk

Rorinvalranus Tallerin

Duplicate Vallen van Joosen

Duplicate Livenna

Rossi von Cossum

Nabi van Rankin

Connor van Cosum

Magnus van Kreeosk

Hannah Tallerin

Kiravalranus Tallerin

Anna

Vita van Reegan

Curran van Lartner

Sari' van Cosum

Neira van Joosen

Ranik van Joosen

Livenna

Vallen van Joosen

Rikerin

Ravenna

Avita

Elana

LIVENNA

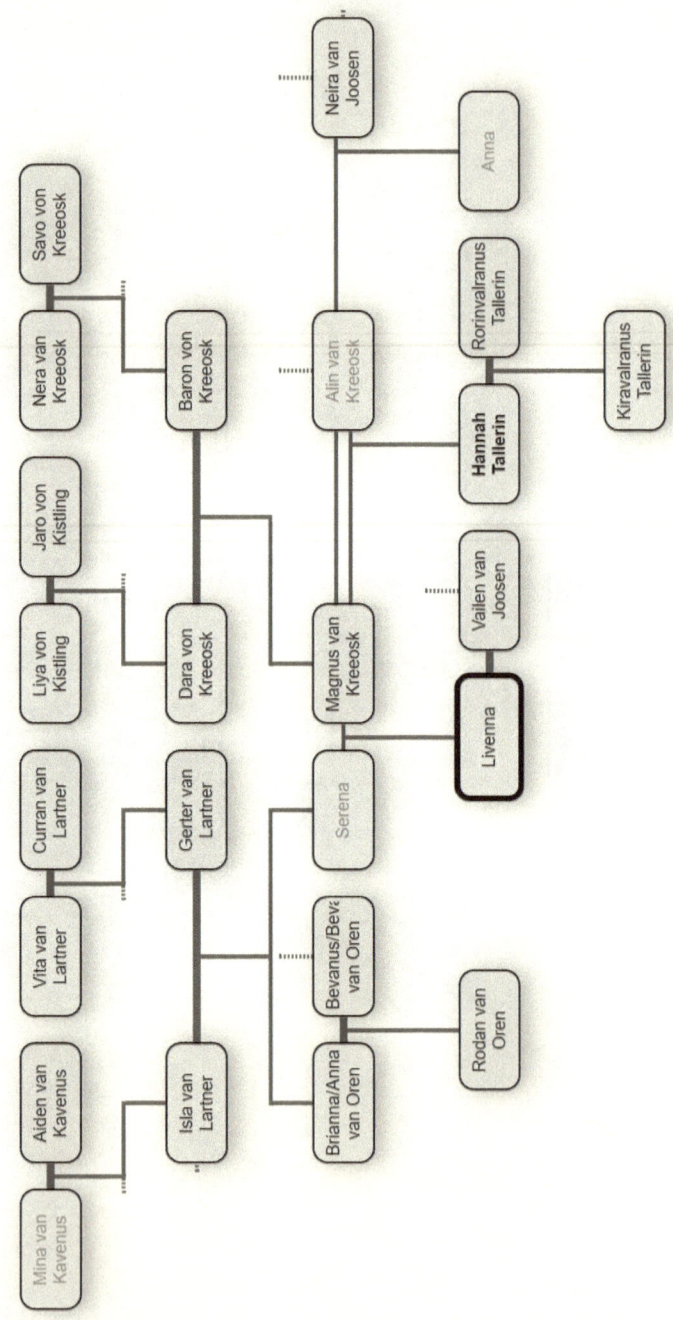

VAN JOOSEN

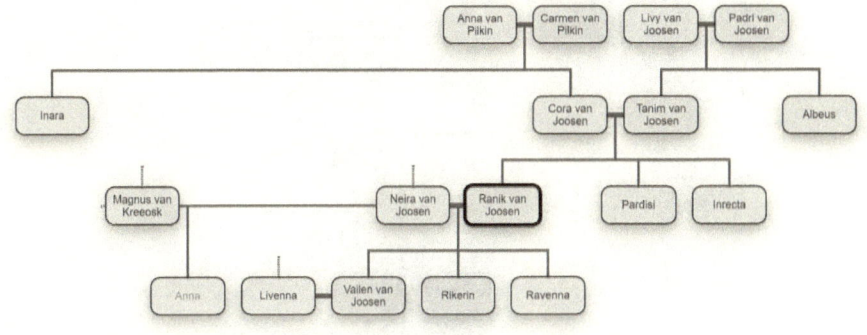

VAN SHERINAK

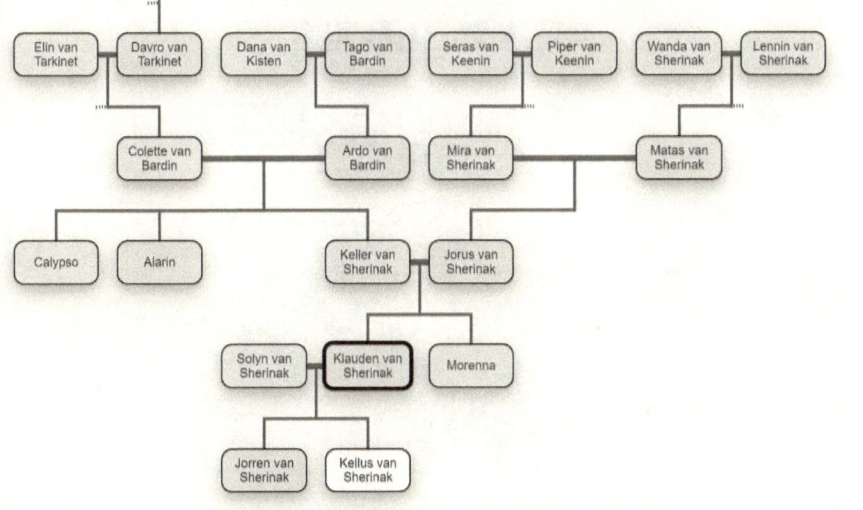

THE SARKOZA

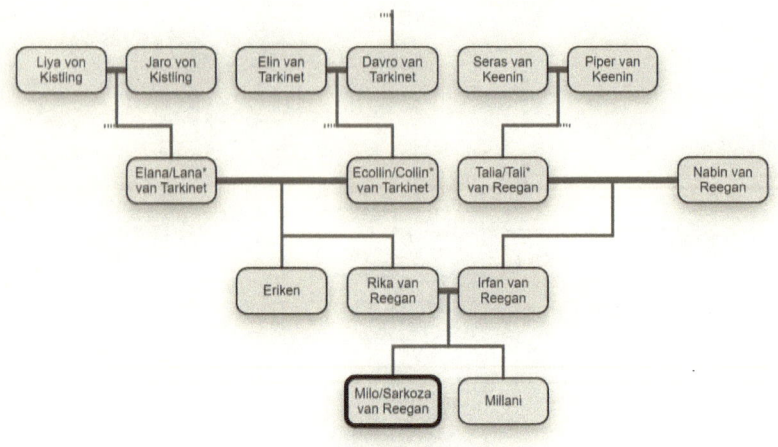

VAN OREN

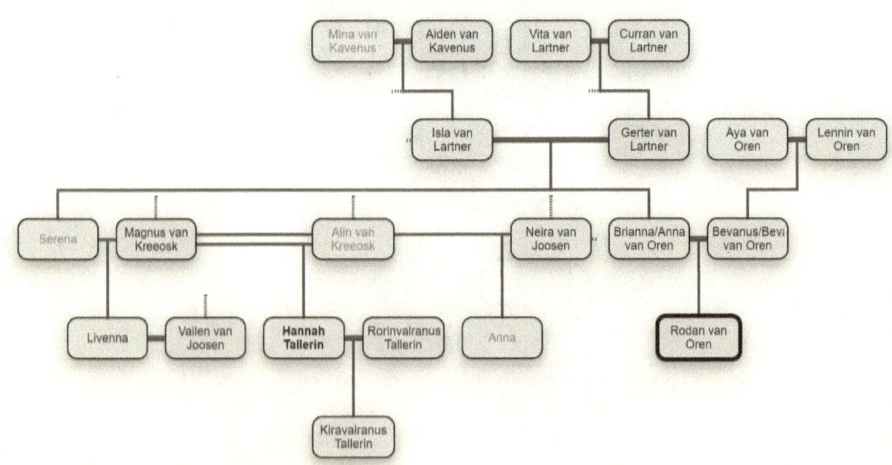

About the Author

Author of the Klauden's Ring Saga and the Conjuring Fascination series, JM Paquette writes fantasy and paranormal romance novels. When she isn't writing, she can be found teaching English to college students as Dr. Paquette or watching her favorite Russian shifter romance movie, *I Am Dragon*. Her areas of expertise include the history of the English language and the intricacies of grammatical rules, but her favorite class to teach is on *Lord of the Rings*. (If you've ever wondered why English is a crazy language, watch her video series on YouTube under Editor JMPaquette!) She enjoys editing manuscripts for academic and creative writers alike, and she adores tabletop roleplaying (THAC0, anyone?) where her halfling ranger/Twi'lek adept/vampire wizard/[insert race and class here] is often underestimated. You can also find her guest co-hosting the podcast Drinking with Authors—even though she doesn't drink, she loves getting to know fellow authors! Check out JM Paquette at authorjmpaquette.com and 4horsemenpublications.com and as Author JM Paquette on Facebook and Instagram.

Connect with JM:
www.authorJMPaquette.com
www.facebook.com/authorjmpaquette/
Email: authorjmpaquette@gmail.com

OTHER BOOKS BY JM PAQUETTE

Klauden's Ring (Klauden's Ring #1)
Solyn's Body (Klauden's Ring #2)
Hannah's Heart (Klauden's Ring #3)
The InBetween (Klauden's Ring #4)

Call Me Forth (Conjuring Fascination Prequel)
Invite Me In (Conjuring Fascination #1)
Keep Me Close (Conjuring Fascination #2)

Heart of Stone (Rock Star Fairy Tales #1)
One Mummy to Go, Please! (Shawarma Warrior King #1) with
Beau Lake

The General Guide to Worldbuilding

BOOK CLUB QUESTIONS

1. "Blood Journal" reveals a young Hannah and Klauden at home in the mountains. How has their relationship changed over time and the events in Klauden's Ring?

2. "In "The River," Hannah is faced with her mortality and fragility. How do you think she handles the limitations of her new human body? How do you think you would adapt in that situation?

3. "The Warrior" shows a different side of Rory. How do you reconcile the exiled prince with the charming rogue Hannah has come to know in Klauden's Ring?

4. Captain Red and Lord Stefan rekindle an old flame. Do you think they could work out their differences and be together? Why or why not? (This is really the "Are you an eternal optimist?" question.)

5.

Discover more at
4HorsemenPublications.com

10% off using HORSEMEN10